ESSENCE OF MAGIC

RUBY MORGAN: BOOK ONE

L.J. RIVERS

ISBN: 978-82-93420-40-8

With love,
for Kristiane, Michael, Storm and Embla

Following a MagX dealer around might not have been the wisest choice to get on Mum's good side. She would have killed me if she knew I was tracking this story. I could hear her now. "Ruby Guinevere Morgan," she would say, then she would give me a scolding glare, the way only she could, and tell me I was 'grounded for life'. Not that she could keep me much longer, now that I had finished year 13, though she could certainly try. She wouldn't like it, but she would have no other choice than to let me test my wings—so to speak. Or so I told myself. Either way, as long as I didn't involve myself in anything having to do with MagX dealers, or worse— Harvesters—Mum might be ok with it.

Yet, here I was, involving myself.

Well, at least I wasn't flaunting my Fae powers to anyone, which was what she feared the most. Granted, she had a point, especially with Harvesters lurking around, although I hadn't heard of any Mags being caught in sleepy Cheshire.

My fingers slid down the camera strap as I narrowed my gaze against the dim light of the early August evening. I looked Craig Hackley up when he had started dealing in Cheshire a couple of weeks back. He was from Liverpool but had relocated down here during summer. There was no way I'd let him go without at least trying to get some useful intel from him. I wasn't stupid enough to believe that all the dealers from the same place knew each other, or that this Craig guy would know anything of use to me, but if there was any chance at all that his business was connected to something about Dad, then I had to find out.

So far I hadn't had much luck. I had been following Craig for the past week, and I had yet to come up with how to approach him without the man running away or whatever else a MagX dealer would do to me on account of sticking my nose where it didn't belong. I was good at that, sticking my nose into things, though I had never had someone actively try to kill me, and I'd rather avoid it if I could. So, I kept my distance and tried to gather the information from afar.

There was a pattern to Craig's movements, which made following him easier, and though he was careful, he was not so careful that someone who went looking for him didn't take notice. It made me think he was fairly new at this, which again made him a terrible lead for finding out about Dad.

I inhaled the warm air and turned my ruby ring around my finger, picturing Dad's gentle smile. Seven years since that horrible night in 2012, and it was still a picture-perfect memory. The ring made me feel closer to him, but his absence was a hole in my heart that I would never be able to mend. If only I could find out the truth, then maybe I could patch myself up enough to live without him. Which was why, these days, I played the part of an aspiring journalist at the local newspaper—out for justice. Only I wasn't sure if I was after justice for the people or mostly for myself. I hoped I was able to do a little of both.

A few strands of red blew over my face in the summer breeze, and I gathered my thick hair at the back of my head, fastening it with a rubber band. The sky was dark with clouds, hiding the sun that was still up somewhere behind them.

There was movement in the alley behind the bar. I had counted on Craig to come here, and he had. I crouched behind a hedge across the road from the bar and brought the camera up. As I zoomed in, the shape of him became clearer as he moved closer to the UV lights of the bar sign. The bass from the music reverberated up my legs as the door swung open and a pair of girls stumbled outside, arm in arm, steadying one another. I squinted, recognising them. Susan had been in my year at school, she was curvy, medium height with a pair of legs that made her look taller than she was. Haley, on the other hand, was a year younger, stocky, with a cute button nose and a bright smile. Neither of them were close friends of mine—not that I had any of those—but I knew them well enough.

The dealer turned to the girls, his hoodie shading his face, and beckoned with two fingers for them to follow. The girls moved sideways, and walked after him into the alley, disappearing from my line of sight.

"Shoot," I muttered. I needed to catch him in the act,

and I had to get a shot of him getting paid while handing over the drugs. I might be out for my own truth, but I also had a story to write. The words of my editor, Logan, whispered at the back of my mind: *Don't ever let a good story die.* As much as I wanted to find out about Dad, I wanted to prove myself and break this story for the Blacon newspaper, a job I was yet to get paid for.

I had written a lot of articles for the Blacon during my internship year, though none as close to my heart as this one. Dealing MagX had become a common thing in the bigger cities, and I wasn't sure Logan would approve of this as breaking news, but I had a feeling I could spin it. And common or not, it was an illegal business, one which had to stop.

Things had got increasingly worse since Dad died. The number of deaths by magical blood was at an all-time high, while the number of users grew accordingly. It was spreading like a vicious rumour. And now, it had come to Cheshire.

I dashed across the street and peered around the corner into the alley. There were four iron sconces mounted on the brick walls. One was broken, the next two shed a dim light, and the last one was flickering, ready to give out. It was enough light to get a decent shot, however, so I raised my camera again, my finger resting on the shutter button as I zoomed back in on Craig and the two girls. I snapped pictures without pause, making sure I didn't miss anything.

The girls were giggling, and Susan brought out a pile of cash from her oversized bag. Craig accepted the cash and handed her something in return. It was hard to tell what, though it was an easy guess. I tried zooming in on what I assumed to be blood panels, hoping it would show up clear enough in at least a picture or two. If Logan wasn't such a cheapskate, he would have agreed to spend a few extra quid on a new camera or at least on a better lens. The camera was ok for beginners, but far from the best fit for this kind of work.

Craig tilted his head at the girls and pulled his hood further down, then turned to walk off. I spun backwards, flung the camera strap over my head and tucked the camera into my backpack. With quick steps, I joined the line outside the bar.

Crap! Why was I still hiding? I wanted to question him. But how? My magic powers were purely defensive, nothing that would intimidate Craig. And if I did manage to hold him long enough to ask him anything, then what? I wasn't going to torture the guy, and at some point, I would have to let him go. By that time, he would know what I was. *Stupid, Ru!*

My pulse quickened as Craig passed the line to The Shade and crossed the street. He wasn't looking my way, though, as he was busy shielding his face and getting out of there.

Once I could no longer see him, I slipped out of the line again and returned to the alley. I walked straight down the cobbled alleyway to find the girls leaning against the brick wall at the end. They were laughing as Susan slid the pieces of a panel apart, her tongue hanging out.

"Hey," I said. "You shouldn't do that."

"Well, if it isn't Miss Goody Two-shoes Morgan," snapped Haley. "Who are you to judge?"

"It's dangerous," I called, stepping closer.

Susan waved one hand at me. "Go away, Ruby. We're just having some fun."

"It could kill you!"

"So could a car. Try living a little. In fact," Susan tilted her head at me, "why don't you try one? I got several interesting samples. How about you try yourself some blood for invisibility."

"There's no such thing," I mumbled.

Haley snickered. "She's not having my superpower, that's for sure."

I wanted to scream at them but took a deep breath instead, and tried my best to compose myself. "My dad died from MagX, so no, I don't want it, and I don't want you to lick that blood either."

The girls stared at me like I was from some different planet, then Susan lifted the panel and gave it a slow lick. She wiped her mouth and shrugged. "What happened to your dad sucks, but he overdosed. We're just having a small taste, is all."

"Yeah, just a taste," Haley agreed, then she licked a panel as well.

I trembled, unable to speak. Before I had time to consider my actions, I hurled myself forwards and grabbed Susan's bag, tossing out the contents. Six panels lay among the make-up, Susan's phone and a pack of chewing gum. I stepped on the panels as hard as I could, a wave of satisfaction washing over me as they crunched and broke beneath my feet.

"You bitch!" Susan stood, her body tense. "I paid a lot of money for those." Her neck craned backwards as she unleashed an ear-splitting cry. The ground shook, and a number of bricks fell from the walls, crashing down. I leaped forwards to avoid getting hit, and pinned Susan to the ground. She laughed bitterly, flexing her fingers to make the cobbles crack and shift around us. Panting, I rolled off her and looked for Haley. She was holding her arms above her head, a large metal beam in her hands, the kind they make to support the weight of roofs. Too large for any human to lift as she did. I glanced upwards. Two similar beams supported the housings, and where the third should have been, there were only two deep wounds in the brick wall on either side.

Super strength!

This was getting out of hand. I had to do something, but what? My powers couldn't stop this. My only hope was that the girls had got short-lived MagX so that it would end on its own, though the norm was for the effects to last at least a few hours.

Susan found her feet again, the ground elevating to lift her up. "You're missing out, Morgan! This is extraordinary!"

Haley bent the beam into a u-shape. "I've never felt this powerful in my life, Suze. Time to go kick my stupid brother's arse!"

They laughed again, this time more shrilly than before.

My feet wouldn't carry me anymore as the ground kept shaking, and my knees hit the cobbles. A rain of bricks tumbled down into the alley, and with no place left to run, I crossed my arms protectively over my head. A sensation of warmth flared up in my veins, and the surge of power blasted through my skin. I watched as the bricks crashed into the force field, while I strained to keep it in place. If the girls hadn't been so preoccupied with testing bought and stolen powers, they would have realised I had magical powers of my own. Real powers. But they weren't paying attention to me anymore.

The final brick dropped, and as it hit the ground, I retracted the magic back under my skin, keeping it alive and close in case I needed it again.

Susan's laugh distorted into a cough. She gasped, her chest heaving for air. What was happening?

"Ha-Haley—" Susan croaked.

Haley, who was busy crushing bricks between her hands, looked back at her friend as Susan tumbled down the slope she had created. The ground stilled, but Susan's body shook, writhing as if trying to fight off an infestation of something that didn't belong. Her mouth frothed and her eyes rolled back.

"Susan!" Haley cried, running over, her thumping steps decreasing in intensity.

The magic was seeping away.

That was fast, a little too fast compared to what I knew about MagX.

I hesitated. The power under my skin swapped places with something calm, a quiet kind of power that was stronger than anything else I possessed. I had to help, no matter the consequences.

The quake had alerted the party next door, and the music had died down. Behind me, a throng of people tried to push through to get a look at the destruction. It didn't matter. It couldn't matter. Exhaling in one long breath, I moved towards Susan and knelt next to her.

I placed my hands over her chest while Haley raised her eyes to me, tears painting her cheeks.

"She's gone," she sobbed. "Her heart has stopped."

I balled my hands to stop the oncoming stream of power.

"Are you sure?" I placed my ear over Susan's heart, then two fingers on her neck. I neither heard nor felt anything. The girl was dead. I backed up, wrapping my arms around myself. It was too late.

"Chief editor coming through," a familiar voice called. "Step aside, please. Local news." Logan squeezed between the thick crowd and climbed over the rubble towards us. He raised his camera and started snapping pictures.

"Logan!" I barked.

He lowered his camera for an instant to meet my gaze.

"A girl is dead," I snapped. "Show some respect, please."

He raised the camera again and snapped another few shots. "The news has to get out," he mumbled. "You been here the whole time?"

"I was," I muttered through clenched teeth.

"Well, then. Looks like we've got ourselves a long night at the office to get this story sorted. I hope you got some good shots."

I shook my head.

"Sorry," I told Haley, standing up.

I looked over at the crowd. Two policemen were passing into the alley and the sound of an ambulance issued close by. This was going to be a long night.

2

I SIPPED AT MY FIFTH POLYSTYRENE CUP OF GREEN TEA. THE warm liquid left a slightly bitter taste on my tongue that I had learned to love, and I shivered briefly as the remnants of tremors finally began to leave my skin. I was all out of lemons, and not for the first time, I wondered why I never started drinking coffee. The police had questioned me for half an hour before I was allowed to leave the scene. Since then, I'd been stuck at the office with Logan peering over my shoulder every five seconds to complain about my choices of words and phrases, though that was about as far as his contribution went. So, I was stuck writing an article about Susan's tragic death while I was still shaky from the ordeal. I wrote down the last sentence and punctuated it with a sigh of relief.

"Can you believe Susan Jones OD'd? Right here in Cheshire?" Logan said, leaning over my shoulder yet again, his breath way too close to my ear. He tapped the screen with his fingers. "I think it's good to go."

I swung my seat around to face him. "Why does anyone take that stuff? Don't they get that it's dangerous?"

"I imagine MagX is somewhat like heroin, Rubes. Only better. People feel like superheroes."

I hated that nickname—Rubes. Coming from him, it sounded totally wrong.

"But they're not," I said. "Susan and Haley looked nothing like superheroes. They both just kind of looked like they had gone mad."

Logan shrugged, grinning.

I stared at him, crossing my arms in disgust. "You too? It's illegal, you know."

"So was weed." Logan wrapped a rainbow-coloured scarf loosely around his neck.

"Still is," I said.

"For now. Besides, it's all about taking the right amount for your body type."

"Susan was tiny, and she only licked one small panel."

"Sure she did. She probably licked a few before you showed up, going for a power boost or something. Judging by that alley, she definitely got her money's worth. Before she died, that is."

I stared at him in disbelief as he scrolled through the pictures he had taken. For once, looking at Logan beat looking at anything else.

"We'll use this one." He pointed at a picture of Haley weeping over Susan's body. It left a bad taste in my mouth, but I was too tired to get into another argument tonight.

"Lock up when you leave?" It was more of a statement—or an order—than a question. He shut down his computer and took his sixpence from the lampshade, adjusting it slightly off-centre on his big head.

The door slammed shut and I turned my attention back to my computer. The words in the article didn't read like my own. And why on earth would Craig, if that was even his real name, be dealing MagX in boring old Cheshire anyway? It was stupid. As I reached to turn off the desk light, I paused. Dad was smiling broadly at me from the single picture I kept on my desk at Blacon. A smaller version of myself sat on his shoulders wearing a red jersey, matching Dad's.

That scumbag Craig had brought the blood from Liverpool. About half a dozen supporters had been arrested for carrying panels at the last game of the season in May, and I had pinned him in a picture in the Echo, showing the police rounding up the perpetrators.

I gazed into Dad's blue eyes. Who would willingly lick a panel of blood for a few hours—or minutes in Haley's and Susan's case—of pleasure, with the possible outcome of death? Certainly not my dad. I refused to believe it. No matter what, I would find the truth. Craig was likely already in the wind, though. Anyone dealing with MagX had an annoying habit of disappearing if things got heated. And this tended to be the kind of heat they shied away from.

Inhaling sharply, I pressed the send button, committing the article to print before shutting down the computer. I hit the main light switch, took a final look at the small newspaper office where I had spent most of my spare time for the past year, then locked the door behind me.

Streams of gold hues from the streetlights pushed through the darkness, shimmering in the droplets teeming down. I yawned, feeling the weight of the day sink in on me. Pulling my hood up, I tucked some red strands under my collar and made my way to the bus stop across from Blacon High School. Despite everything, I had to smile at the memories. My first kiss had been on the football field behind the school. It was awkward, his tongue filling my mouth, wet and sloppy. Mike rarely looked my way these days, which was fine by me. A lot of firsts had taken place in that school, and it had all come to an end. Now, I was free to do what I wanted—assuming Mum would grant me that freedom.

My jeans stuck to my skin as the moisture seeped through the denim. I looked down into the pleading eyes of a drenched orange kitten, rubbing itself against my leg.

"Hey, kit," I said quietly.

The kitten purred, the vibrations tickling my ankle. My sneakers were soaked too, but I didn't care. The poor animal, however, looked like it could use some shelter. It was too young to be out here on its own.

"You live around here?" I asked, not actually expecting a reply. Still, the kitten looked like it understood. It made a couple more turns around my feet then sauntered off, balancing on the edge of the pavement.

A pair of beams from the bus's headlights lit up the corner of Auckland Road. The bus was moving fast. Too fast. I tried waving, hoping the driver would see, but it wasn't slowing down.

The kitten leaped off the pavement and into the street.

"Get back here," I yelled. "Now!"

The kitten turned its head at me, but stopped in the middle of the road while the bus headed straight for it. Stupid animal.

"No. Get away from there."

My pulse pounded in my chest and the warm sensation of magic bubbled forth in my veins. I stretched my fingers out but hesitated. I wasn't supposed to, and this was hardly the same as what had gone down earlier tonight. The roar from the bus engine filled the air. I had to. With a flick of my hands, an orb of white light formed in my palms before I pushed it towards the kitten. A nearly invisible shield wrapped around the animal. The side of the bus rammed into the force field, sending it flying onto the grass on the other side just as the bus rushed past the bus stop, showering me in water.

"Idiot," I muttered as I ran across the street.

My fingers danced over the small animal, and the force field disappeared as I cradled it in my arms.

"Why did you do that?" I wasn't sure if I was talking to the kitten or myself. I shifted my eyes around, but most lights were off in the nearby houses. Not a person to be seen on the street either. It had been a subtle use of magic and I had acted on instinct. There had been no time to consider the ramifications of what I was doing. It wasn't likely that anyone had noticed me at all. Still, my mum's words were a constant reminder at the back of my mind: *Harvesters can be anyone and anywhere. We cannot risk being seen.*

The kitten snuggled in my embrace and I wrapped it

under my coat. I couldn't leave it out here, and I shouldn't be knocking on doors this late. I would have to look for the owner in the morning.

"I guess you're coming with me. It's a long way home but that was the last bus tonight."

I took a shortcut down to Melverly Drive, hurried past the last houses and through the trees leading to the fields beyond. My feet sank into the wet soil, but crossing Mr Hayworth's land would still save me time. The furball hidden under my jacket clawed at my chest, and I sped up as much as I could.

It took me a good long hour before I could finally push open the door of the old brick house. It creaked more than I liked but I hoped it wasn't enough to wake Mum. A light switched on in the living room, and Mum leaned forward in her armchair. No need to worry about being quiet after all.

She clutched a piece of paper in her hand, wrinkling her forehead. "You're terribly late."

"Sorry, Mum. The bus driver didn't see me."

Mum placed the paper on the coffee table next to her, smoothing the edges with her fingers. "And when were you going to tell me?"

I shook myself like a wet cat, my clothes dripping into pools on the floor. The logo on top of the paper was one I had looked at a hundred times over the past few weeks. White Willow University. In London. I had wanted to wait, though it seemed we were getting into this now.

"I'm spent. Can we please talk about it in the morning?"

"No."

I unzipped my jacket and placed the kitten gently on the floor before kicking my shoes off and carrying them into the warmth of the laundry room. I removed my drenched socks and jeans, swapping them out with a pair of sweatpants, then pulled off my soaked top and changed into my favourite red t-shirt with YNWA written on it. I proceeded to grab a towel and wrapped it around my dripping wet hair before I walked past Mum to the kitchen. In the cupboard over the sink, I found a bowl and filled it with milk.

"Here, kit. Drink. I need to talk to my mum a bit, but you can sleep in my room after." I left the bowl with the kitten, and dumped down in the chair opposite Mum, her judgmental gaze burning holes in me.

"I want to go," I said.

"We have been over this, love. It's not safe."

"It's as safe as anywhere else. I wrote an article today about a MagX overdose right here in Cheshire. Susan Jones. I was there when it happened."

Mum closed her eyes briefly, sinking back in the chair. "By the Lady Herself, I'm sorry you had to see that." She angled toward me. "It's spreading fast, I know. All the more reason to stay clear of trouble. What if you were spotted?"

"I'm careful, Mum. No one knows about my Fae persuasion. Why would they? I've hardly used my powers over the past six years." Not that I hadn't wanted to. It was hard to suppress the magical energy inside of me. It was always present, lingering and whispering in my veins.

Mum's expression softened, and her breathing slowed. The sorrow of losing Dad had never quite left the lines in her face. And as her brow furrowed, it was as if the sadness of his death spilled out all over again.

"You were only twelve," Mum mumbled. "Too young to lose a parent. But if Dennis's death taught us anything, it is that we have to stay hidden. It's not what I want for you, but I want you alive more than anything."

"I know." I folded a hand over Mum's forearm. "But I'm nineteen now. There's no future for me in Cheshire. I would die from boredom before any Harvester could get to me." The kitten sneaked up on me and curled up by my feet.

Mum tilted her head at it. "Taking home strays now, are we?"

"The poor thing was almost run over by the bus. It would have died, and—" I had said too much. Me and my big mouth.

"Ruby Guinevere Morgan!"

"No one saw. I promise."

"That settles it. You're not going to London. Not on my watch."

I gritted my teeth. "You have to let me live. I'll dry up in this place, and you'll hate the person I'll become as much as I will. It's not like you won't see me. You can visit, and I'll be home for vacations." I took a deep breath and tried to soften my voice. "Please, Mum. Dad would have said yes. I know he would."

I knew I was right. Dad had always had faith in me. Why didn't Mum?

"Your dad would want you safe, darling."

I cradled the kitten in my arms as I stood.

"I'm going. Upstairs for now." I stomped out of the living room. It didn't matter if I was here or in London, Harvesters were everywhere, and there was no place safe from them.

3

I could almost hear the seconds ticking. I really shouldn't snooze the alarm again, but knew I would. Logan just had to deal with me coming in late today. If I went downstairs now, Mum would still be in the kitchen, and I had no intention of speaking to her yet.

Not until she agreed to let me go to London.

If only I were a bit more rebellious. After all, I didn't really need my Mum's approval. Maybe I should just pop online and accept my spot? Get it over with, and take the fight later.

But no. That wasn't the deal, what we had agreed on when we moved up here. Mum's words were still so vivid in my memory: 'It's just you and me now, Ru. We need to work as a team. We owe it to your father'.

Instead, I would work on the right arguments and deliver a convincing sales pitch during dinner. Any half-decent journalist should be able to find the right words. And wasn't I already past half-decent?

The door downstairs closed, and seconds later

Mum's old Ford Fiesta coughed its way up the gravel road, heading north to Saughall and her job at the clinic. I grabbed the phone as the alarm was about to start singing its cheerful tune, which today was even more annoying. When I sat up, a small orange ball of fur crawled from under the sheet and onto my lap.

"You little beauty," I said, almost purring as much as the kitten. "Let's see if we can find some food, shall we?"

This time I was almost certain I could hear the little cat reply. Oh, well—it was just purring a little louder.

The scent of eggs and bacon infused the house as I walked out of my room. Mum had left me a full plate of breakfast on the kitchen table, but it would have to wait while I fed Kit, as I had now named it. I hadn't checked if it was a boy or a girl, and Kit would do well for both, I figured. While I finished my meal, the kitten ate almost a full slice of bread, which I had cut into tiny pieces and soaked in milk. I would have to get proper food for it when I got back home from—

"Holy Lady," I moaned. "I can't very well bring you to work with me, and you really can't be here alone all day."

I scooped Kit up and went outside. I put him in the little basket on the front of my bike, and lay my jacket on top of him, gently so as not to suffocate the poor thing. If I rode slowly and carefully, it would be fine. The kitten stared at me with large eyes as I snapped a few pictures of him to use for the 'kitten found' posts I was going to have to create for my social media accounts. I might even go old school and print a few posters.

The ride south towards Cheshire went well, if one

considered about a dozen stops to convince the small cat to stay in the basket. Eventually he quieted, submitting to the travel arrangements, and at almost eight thirty, I steered the bike onto Melverly Drive.

The street was slowly buzzing with school children and parents, one more tired than the other as they stumbled out of the identical redbrick houses. I liked the quaint town, and this street in particular, but with the acceptance to uni, it all seemed so mundane. So boring. I wanted to do more with my life than stay here forever, and now an opportunity had presented itself.

I parked my bike next to the fence surrounding the house at the very end of the road and picked up Kit from the basket. I opened the gate, and as I walked halfway to the front door, the old woman had already spotted me from her kitchen window. Her big smile had greeted me exactly like this ever since the first time I walked on the cobbled pathway up to the white door many years ago.

"Good morning, child," crooned Mrs Wellington as I came into the kitchen. "Not at work yet? Oh my, you're not ill, are you? I've told you a million times to wear a scarf on that bike, dear."

"No, Mrs Wellington, I'm fine." I smiled. Her concern for me warmed my heart. Not having any contact with my grandparents, though they remained alive and well back in Wales, Mrs Wellington had become the perfect substitute. "I just had to ... arrange something before work."

I opened my arms enough for Mrs. Wellington to meet Kit.

"Now isn't that a little gem," said the old woman.

"Let me guess. He followed you home, and now you face some practical consequences, eh?"

Of course, Mrs Wellington read all that in a few seconds. I guessed it came with age and experience.

"Well, yes. And I'm not sure it's a he or a she yet," I replied.

"This little charmer is a boy, all right," Mrs Wellington said, extending her arms.

I gave her the kitten. "How can you tell?"

"Just his way of looking at things." Mrs Wellington winked at me. "Run along now, and rest assured that old Lucinda will take good care of him. What's his name?"

"Kit. And thank you so much. I'll be back by half six at the latest, and I'll bring cat food."

"Yes, yes," said the old woman, already lost in the little kitten's eyes.

"So, you finally remembered where you should be today?" Logan said with pretend disappointment.

"Sorry," I muttered as I sat down at my desk. "I had a minor emergency. Figured I wouldn't waste time calling you, so I just pedalled my ass off instead."

"Ok." He squinted for a second, dragging the word slightly upwards at the end. "Anyway, what are you working on today?"

What story do you want to steal, you mean? was what I wanted to say.

He never paid any attention to my stories or leads until I had written whatever piece I was working on. Then

—depending on his mood—he would either post it under his name or let me use my own byline. Not surprisingly, my best articles were always bylined by *Logan Whelk*.

"The manager at the factory hasn't confirmed anything yet," I said while I uploaded the picture of Kit to various social media platforms, "but I'm pretty sure we'll hear something today. If they get the contract with the Chinese, it will—"

"Yes, that's fine," Logan interrupted. "It will be good for Cheshire and taxes and all that. Could you give me fifteen hundred words by lunch?"

"Sure."

Logan made a pistol with his index finger and thumb, lowering his thumb just as he made a clicking sound with his tongue. He winked at me with a stupid grin on his face.

"You're the best intern I've had, Rubes. What plans do you have after this? University, I presume?"

"Journalism, yes. If I get in, of course."

Logan tilted his head slightly. "But admissions must have been weeks ago? What's today, the third?"

I tapped the date on the article on my computer screen.

"Right, August 5th, of course," Logan said. "So, what's your plan?"

"I'm weighing my options," I said, turning to the computer screen.

As usual, Logan's antennae were out of commission. He leaned on my desk. "I could make a call if you like. I think my name has some pull in Chester." He angled closer, lowering his voice even though no one else was around. "Let's talk about it over lunch. Maybe I can help you decide."

I pulled back and looked up at him. "Uhm, thanks, but I don't think I'll be going to university in Chester."

"What, Warrington? Don't say you're thinking of West Cheshire, Rubes? Those hacks wouldn't know the first thing about real journalism!"

Like you would? I almost laughed in his face.

"I haven't decided yet, that's all. Listen, Logan, I have an appointment at lunchtime. I'm meeting coach Brown about the latest signings and his plans for next season." Besides, I needed to get my mind off last night's events.

Logan waved me off. "Well, if you're thinking of West Chester or Warrington, you'd be way better off working here. How about I promote you from intern to a permanent journalist position?"

He trailed his finger lightly up the seams of my top, then brushed a lock of hair from my collar bone back over my shoulder. "We make a great team already. Think of what lies ahead if we worked," he paused for a second, "closer."

It was a reflex, pure instinct, but in hindsight, I would have done it even if I'd had all the time in the world to think about it. The impact with his cheek sent a tremor up my forearm, leaving a red mark on one side of his face. I briefly regretted that I hadn't turned my ring around on my finger, so the little ruby would have scratched him as well.

"You self-righteous frigid bitch!" he snarled. "What the hell was that?"

"That was me saying no to your offer, you perv!"

He pulled back, and for a second I thought he was going to take a swing at me as payback, but the hand he raised was for himself—rubbing his cheek. He was clearly pissed, however.

"Ungrateful little wench! Pack your things and get the hell out. You're fired."

"You can't fire me," I snapped. "I quit.

4

"WHY ON EARTH WOULD YOU DO SUCH A THING?" MUM stood by the kitchen table, her arms crossed. "I thought a few more months down the road you could get a proper job there, or at least enough experience to apply to other newspapers?"

"It wasn't right, ok? Just leave it. It's done." I swallowed another spoonful of soup, and tore a piece off the olive bread. With my mouth full, I at least didn't have to speak.

Mum, however, was not done at all. "It was only a couple of days ago you said you liked it there, that you wanted to become a journalist. And what about that factory story you've been working on?"

To hell with mouthfuls of bread. "I said leave it," I muttered, breadcrumbs spilling into the bowl of soup. I pushed the chair back so fast it thumped to the floor, but I left it. It was just a bloody chair, for heaven's sake. Striding up the stairs, two steps at a time, I rushed into my room, almost slamming the door. I thought better of it, and left it open for Kit to join me.

Tears had already gathered in my eyes and I couldn't blink them all away. Soon, small rivers flowed down my cheeks. I lay back on the bed and prompted Kit to jump onto my chest. The little ball of fur wiggled his way close to my face, tickling my skin, almost burying itself under my long red hair.

"Sorry, little one," I whispered, a small laugh forming in my throat. "I'm not ready to accept any men right now, even one as cute as you."

I checked my phone briefly. There were several hearts and a few replies attached to my posts about Kit, but no one claimed him as theirs. Three soft knocks on the door made me sit up, and I pocketed the phone again.

"Ru, honey?"

"Leave me alone!" I called.

"Come on. Let's talk, all right?"

The door opened slowly, and Mum inserted her head, strawberry-blonde curls falling over her face. "About all and nothing?"

I sighed. "Fine."

Mum sat on the chair by my old oak desk. She let her finger run down a picture of me and my dad. Swallowing visibly, she looked back at me.

"I'm just so scared, love. If anything were to happen to you, I would never forgive myself."

"You can't protect me all my life. That's not a life I want."

"Of course I can protect you." Mum sat beside me, her warmth nearly tangible in the air as she folded her hand over mine. The little kitten bounced to his feet and started to climb the newcomer. "I just can't hold your hand all the time. I know that. Still, letting go is hard."

"As it should be. But you have to let me find my own way. Make my own mistakes."

Mum tilted her head and her blue eyes widened. A small spark, reminiscent of starbursts, appeared in her irises. "Like slapping your boss?"

I gasped. "You—you know?"

"Just because I never practice magic in public, and never intend to, doesn't mean I can't. A mother must be allowed to have a tiny peek into her daughter's heart now and again. Can you forgive me?"

Mum had intruded on my thoughts. However much I wanted to be upset about that, I understood why she had done it. A part of me was even glad, as it prevented me from having to say the words out loud.

"He was—he wanted to—"

Mum held her hand up and nodded. "I didn't read your mind, love. I just saw that slap, and maybe something about your ring?" She smiled and poked me in the ribs.

"Stop it," I said and laughed.

She wiped the remaining tears from my cheek.

"But yes, Dad would have loved it if I scratched that moron's face with it."

"That's not why he gave it to you," Mum started. "Still, I think you're right. Dennis would not have let it pass. He would probably be halfway to Blacon Press as we speak to deal with that misogynistic creep." She drew her breath, held it for a few seconds and slowly let it out. "And I think you're right about Dad letting you go to university, too," she said.

"I know I am," I whispered.

"Here," said Mum, putting her palm up on the bed next to me.

I took it, and an immediate rush of magic coursed through my veins that was not my own. Colours of red, blue and yellow danced before my eyes, even though I had unwittingly closed them. The colours started forming into the shape of something—a human? And then he stood there, right in front of me. Tears threatened to spill out all over again. He looked as real as if he was there. Dad!

"I agree with your dad," my mum's voice sang in my head. Only, she didn't say the words as much as convey them to me. Dad smiled at her and nodded before the vision of him evaporated and Mum let go of my hand.

"Let's go sign that letter."

"What was that?" I said, marvelling at her as I opened my eyes.

"As I said, a mother is allowed a few tricks. We are Fae, after all." Mum stood, holding her arms out. "So, shall we?"

I beamed with joy and leapt from the bed, throwing my arms around her. "Thank you, Mum. Thank you!"

I sent off a silent thank you to Dad as well, reminding him that one day I would find out the truth about his death.

5

ALTHOUGH I HADN'T BEEN DANCING ON TOP OF ANY CARS or stumbling out of any bars lately—or ever, really—I was belting out the words together with my childhood heroes. Who would have thought I'd be singing along-side the Jonas Brothers again? They weren't nearly as cute now as ten-year-old me had thought when they ruled the Disney Channel, though. Kit had climbed onto the kitchen top and stared at me in disbelief.

"I'm a sucker for you," I sang, grabbing him and holding him up to my face. "Yes, I am, sweetie. I'm such a sucker for you." I buried my nose in his fur, his purring vibrating against my skin.

Mum peeked through the kitchen door. "How's it going?"

"Mum! Get out! I'm not done yet."

I hurled a tiny force field at the door, pushing it shut. Kit wiggled himself free and scurried under the table as Mum's screaming laughter faded. This was going to be a great night, albeit a sad one as well, as it was our last together before I left for London and uni.

In the oven, the baby carrots and broccolini stems had got that shiny caramelisation I was aiming for. I'd give them a couple more minutes. Just enough time to finish the dipping sauce. I cracked an egg in a bowl, making quite a mess of it. My hands were covered with egg yolk, but I didn't care as I danced across the floor to the fridge to get the Dijon mustard. A splash of lemon juice joined the egg, mustard and a clove of garlic, and I poured it all into the blender.

I heard a tiny clink, but it didn't register in my brain until it was too late. My plan was to drizzle the olive oil ever so slowly into the egg mix until it emulsified into a creamy garlic mayonnaise. Or aioli, as the guy in the YouTube video on my phone had called it.

"What the—?" A loud rattling told me something was wrong down in the mix. I let go of the button and stared at my hand.

"No, no, no!" This could not be happening!

My fingers must have been greased by the egg yolk, causing my ring to slip into the mix. I swallowed hard and grabbed a fork from the drawer. Carefully, I managed to fish the most precious memory I had of my dad out of the bowl. *Please don't be broken,* I prayed. The Jonas Brothers claimed to be "a sucker for me", but I was the one who felt like a sucker.

I rinsed the ring under the tap and dried it on my apron—blowing at it to get every drop of water off. Through a steadily thickening veil of tears, I tried to examine it, but couldn't see it clearly. I wiped my eyes and turned the ring back and forth.

"Please be ok," I moaned while Kit rubbed against my legs, meowing and purring.

"Ruby?" Mum said, knocking at the door. "Are you ok in there? Need any help?"

"Everything's under control," I lied. "Finishing touches now."

She sounded anxious to help, as I knew she wanted to. Cooking was not my strong suit, but I wanted to make this last meal special.

Last winter, we had spent almost an entire Saturday mounting ceiling lights in the kitchen, laughing and swearing but determined to show the world—or ourselves, at least—that we could manage. Now, I stood on one of the kitchen chairs, holding the ring up to the flush LED light. The red ruby acted as a prism, sending rays of all colours out of it, and the metal seemed to have maintained its shape. Thank the Lady!

"Five minutes," I shouted as I jumped off the chair. "Open the wine."

"Yeah, right," I heard Mum mutter.

I breathed out a silent, thankful sigh and slid the ring back on my finger. A cramping sensation in my stomach slowly let go.

"I think I dodged a bullet there," I whispered to Kit.

What was that smell? The vegetables! I rushed to the oven, and without thinking pulled the baking tray with the carrots and broccolini straight out and threw it on the kitchen top. I turned them just as frantically as I had the ring seconds earlier, and although the crisis was way less of a crisis, I was very happy to see that they were not burnt. Dark, yes, but not burnt. I hoped.

Slowly, it dawned on me. I turned my palm,

35

expecting to see a black or red line on it. The scorching hot tray had to have left a burn mark.

But no, my hand was unharmed. *Wow*, I thought. I must have acted so fast, it didn't register. "Fastest hands in the west," I said to Kit, who tilted his head at the crazy Fae.

Seven minutes later, I carried the plates out on the grass, where we had put the patio table and chairs.

Mum smiled. "It smells delicious. What is it?"

"Tonight, madame," I said, doing my best French chef impression, "we 'ave a filet mignon with duchess potatoes and spiced butter, served with oven-roasted vegetables and Mediterranean aioli."

Mum clapped enthusiastically. "That's amazing, Ruby."

"'Oo is diz Ruby, madame? I am Chef Bouillabaisse."

"But of course," Mum said, suppressing a laugh.

We dug into the meal with great enthusiasm. The food was good. Not great, but way better than anything I'd ever made before. Mum loved it, although I suspected she lay a bit more praise on it than necessary. Still, the night was every bit as nice as I'd hoped for. We talked and laughed, Mum sharing a few stories from my childhood. None that I hadn't heard dozens of times before, but I had no intention of stopping her. Besides, I loved to hear them, as they usually involved Dad. I basked in the glory of it all as the light in the sky dimmed and the stars came out, casting glimmering reflections on the pond behind our house. I was excited to leave, but I was going to miss it.

As I stood to clear the table, Mum lay her hand on mine. "Leave it. We're not quite done celebrating yet."

"We're not?"

"We're just getting started. Stay here." Mum darted back into the house, returning moments later with a basket full of who knew what. "Here. One for you and one for me." She handed me a pen and a notebook.

"We're writing travel plans? Poetry perhaps?" I teased.

Mum took my free hand and guided me to the edge of the pond, where we sat on the grass. She put her pen and notebook next to her, then brought up four thick white candles. She lit them and placed each inside its own candle house, before arranging them by the edge of the pond. The light shimmered on the water, dancing alongside the reflection of the stars. A swarm of fireflies joined in, gliding soundlessly just above the surface. Humans might not have magic, but this came pretty close.

"Now," Mum said. "I want you to write down three wishes. And not any wishes. They have to be genuine and true, and they have to be personal."

"Why?" I asked.

"It's an ancient Fae tradition." Mum smiled solemnly. "It dates back to before our time here on Earth, all the way to Avalonian times."

"Avalon," I murmured. I loved hearing about it, but I never pushed. Mum rarely spoke about the world where Magicals descended from. I think it made her sad to know that it was lost while reminding her of all the pain and suffering Magical beings had endured over the centuries we had been on Earth.

"My mum did this with me when I left home to go to Liverpool, where I met your dad."

I wrinkled my nose at her. "You mean the mother who then shunned you for, how did she say, *breeding with a worthless human?*"

"That's the one. You have to understand, darling. My parents are Pure Fae, and strong believers of keeping our bloodline pure as well. My dad has it in his head that if we stay pure, then perhaps one day we might find our way back to Avalon. Humans have mistreated Magicals for so long, and my parents have not had the best of experiences dealing with them. Whenever magic was discovered, humanity's first instinct was always fear. These days, with almost everything out in the open, it's more evident than ever before. And fear is not a long way from hate."

"But you're their daughter." I could never understand how my grandparents could shut their daughter out of their lives completely. Then again, I had never met them.

"And I always will be."

My arms were crossed tightly over my chest. "We don't choose who to love."

"We don't, but we do make choices on how to act." She waved her pen in my face. "Now, wipe that frown off, and forget about those old Fae folk. Let's celebrate instead."

I lowered my shoulders and nodded, then brought my pen up and tapped it against Mum's in a toast. "So, madame, three wishes, no?"

"Yes, Chef Bouillabaisse. Exactly so."

I pursed my lips in thought. What did I wish for? World peace? The end of hunger and sickness? I did, but it didn't seem like those were the kinds of wishes Mum intended me to make. So, then what?

I lifted my eyes from the blank paper to watch my mum scribbling away. At least someone was in touch with their inner wishes. Returning my attention to the task at hand, I tried to dig deep. I wanted Mum to be happy without me, to find her true purpose. Yes, that would be my first wish. Then, what else? I wanted to become a renowned journalist, I guess, but I dismissed the thought instantly. It wasn't the right kind of wish either, so what was?

I wanted to have friends. That was a real wish, something I had wanted for a long time. Not that I'd never had friends, but I never had true friends, the kind I could share everything with, the kind that didn't judge me for what I was. That would be my second wish. Now for my third wish. I shook my head as I came up empty-handed.

"I can't think of a third, Mum."

"Search your heart, darling, and stop analysing. Clear your mind and picture what you want in life." She gave me a tilt of the head. "It will come to you."

I took a deep breath and tried to let go of all my concerns and worries for the future. What did I want? It came to me then, and I scribbled it down in bold letters on the page.

"Done."

"Perfect." Mum tore out the piece of paper she had written her wishes on. "Now, follow my lead."

With my own piece of paper in my hands, I watched and repeated her moves, folding the papers together into the smallest square we could manage. We joined our wishes and formed a force field around them before carefully pushing it out into the water. It floated into the centre of the pond, dipping gently on the surface.

The notes from a song I had heard a thousand times over began trickling out of my mum. Her voice was as always pitch-perfect, but tonight it was filled with raw emotion and it sounded nothing short of divine. She nodded at me, and I reluctantly joined in. My voice was fine, though compared to hers, I might as well have been a crow. Still, I made my best effort, the words imprinted deep in my memories. It was a song about the Fae, about Avalon—a land far from this one. All in all, it was mostly a prayer to the Lady of the Lake.

As we sang, the water began spiralling around the circular force field, water washing softly outwards and over the edges, spilling onto the grass. The light intensified as it was joined by glimmering shafts of gold and ruby colours.

I took my mum's hand and she squeezed it gently. Around us, the crickets provided us with their natural instruments, and though the birds should have been asleep, a choir of chirps became our backup singers. The light flooded out into the night, illuminating the entire garden, shifting beams flowing onto the trees. The ringlets of water grew before the contents of the lake shot up and cascaded out like a fountain, raining over our wishes, which were now levitating in the air. The water then fell over the force field, swallowing the wishes into its embrace. The shimmering orb evaporated in a flash of light before the water rushed back down into the pond, gushing back in a downward spiral before it levelled out. The song ended with the last splash, and both the crickets, the birds, and the water went back to being as still as it had been before we sang.

"We thank you," Mum whispered to the pond.

I wrapped my arms around her. "Our wishes are gone."

She laughed softly into my ear. "Not gone. They are with the Lady of the Lake."

"Not really, though," I said quietly.

She leaned back, eyeing me. "We may not be able to travel back and forth between here and the magical island of Avalon. But She, She transcends worlds. I know in my heart that She has heard our call."

Mum sounded like she somehow believed there was still a doorway back to Avalon. But she couldn't possibly think that. She had said herself that Avalon was lost. Staring at her, I realised that Mum meant every word, and I wasn't about to argue, so instead I fell back into the hug.

Tomorrow, I would leave. If I were to believe my mum, and she was usually right, then maybe the Lady of the Lake had heard us. It gave me comfort to think that Mum would find her purpose without me, whatever that would be. And perhaps I would find my purpose, too.

6

THE LARGE IRON GATES WERE WROUGHT INTO WILLOW branches at the top, with the university motto underneath. *Scientia, amicitia et virtus*—knowledge, friendship and virtue. I hoped those words would come true.

I took a deep breath, adjusted my backpack and tightened my grip on the handle of the chequered wheeled suitcase before striding onto White Willow University campus. It was as if I had tumbled down the rabbit hole into another world. It was so different from the busy streets I had seen from the bus on my way from the tube station. I remembered the campus from the pictures on the website, but seeing it with my own eyes was entirely different. It didn't quite look like it belonged in London.

The scent of lilacs tickled my nose, almost covering the smell of the countless number of pints being consumed outside the pub nearby and on the lawn beyond, which spread over the size of several football fields, surrounding a lake.

Several different buildings stood at odd places throughout the grounds, a couple of modern-looking student houses towering along the walls that went all around campus, according to the map on my phone. There was even a chapel, a library and more student houses further away. The loud chatter from the numerous students who had gathered in the midday sun made my lips form a broad smile. This was nothing like Cheshire.

I pressed my thumb to my phone and swiped sideways until I found the White Willow University app, scrolling down to tap the map icon. Pinching my fingers to zoom in on my location, I tried to make sense of my surroundings. I had to find the Accommodations Office, get settled, then maybe head over to the events of Freshers' Week, if I could manage to find my way around this place.

"Looking for something?" A girl wearing a layered white dress stood in front of me with her phone raised, taking pictures. Her golden hair was pulled back into a high ponytail, the ends dancing between her shoulder blades. Combined with her outfit, she looked like I imagined a Greek goddess would.

"The Accommodations Office?"

"Cool. You're moving into campus today?"

Duh. What gave it away? "Yes. I'm moving into—" I glanced at the map. "Craydon Court."

The girl snapped a picture and showed me all her perfect, white teeth. "That's my house too. I'm Jeannine Lune, but everyone calls me Jen."

She spoke perfect English, but the way she

pronounced her name and almost made the h in house silent hinted at a French heritage.

"Ruby. Ruby Morgan."

"Awesome. Love your name. Can I take your picture? You're perfect for my Insta."

"Uhm." I smiled awkwardly, thinking about how dishevelled I looked. I hadn't showered or brushed my teeth since yesterday, as my train had left so early that I couldn't be bothered this morning. Not that anyone could smell me from looking at a picture. Sod it. Who cared, anyway?

"Sure. What's your Insta about?"

"*Hashtag Feminism*. You fit the profile." Jen winked and pressed her thumb repeatedly on the phone before she seemed satisfied. "The Accommodations Office is past Brady's Breakfast, and behind Raven Court. Can't miss it if you head through the lilac archway."

"Thank you."

"See you around, Red."

"See ya."

I turned away from Jen and continued along a walkway past the lake, making a mental note that this would be a good place for my morning run. A boy and a girl stood underneath a white willow, close to the edge of the water, shaded by the canopy above. They were both wearing matching uni jumpers. A pair of red sneakers on the girl's feet stood out against the green grass. The boy had his hood up, spikes of brown hair sticking out. He kept turning his head this way and that.

I squinted. What were they doing?

The girl handed something over, covering one hand

with the other. As the item passed between them, a spear of light hit the plastic panel in the boy's hand. I bit down on my tongue, nearly dropping all my stuff and sprinting down to the pair of them. There was no escaping it. And though I was well aware that MagX had become almost as common as weed in London, I had hoped to avoid it— at least for a while. Every bone in my body told me to run over and grab that blood panel away from them.

I slowed my steps. Could I?

A flick of my hand, and I could send a force field across the lawn to push that panel into the water, instantly contaminating it and rendering it useless. I looked around at the buzz of other students all over the campus, then kicked my heel into the suitcase.

Don't be stupid, Ruby. You're not alone. Mum had been very clear about the need to hide who I was and the things I could do. It was dangerous enough in Cheshire, let alone here. There could easily be a Harvester at any corner, on the lookout for Magicals. However much I wanted to, I couldn't risk it. Besides, I didn't want to repeat my experience with Susan and Haley. I made a mental image of those red shoes, and that girl dealing magical blood. I had no idea how, but I would find out who was distributing the drugs and somehow shut them down. Dad's death would not go unpunished, and this was the only way I knew to honour his memory.

Turning my back to the willow, I sped up again and willed myself to walk away. It was simply something I would have to get used to. At least it might be easier than I thought to find both users and dealers. And as long as I didn't let any Harvesters close enough to discover who—or what—I was, I would be safe.

Key and key card in hand, I climbed the steps to the second floor of Craydon Court. The front door to number four was kept ajar by a pair of colourful Converses, and a couple of girls sat on the porch, sharing a smoke. A young man in a blue overall, a toolbox in one hand and a large keychain on his belt, tapped one of the girls on the shoulder.

"There's a designated smoking area down there." He pointed to the corner of the small garden by the entrance to Craydon Court. "I have enough that needs fixing, I don't need to collect cigarette butts all day long."

The girl held up a beer can and dropped the cigarette end into it. "Problem solved." She grinned at the janitor.

He shook his head and walked off. The girls giggled, then waved at me as I pushed my way into my new home. The living space was empty and most doors in the hallway were shut. One was propped open, however, allowing The Killers to belt out "Smile Like You Mean It" into every nook and cranny.

I peeked into the room. A short girl with round glasses and thick, dark hair sat on the windowsill, immersed in what looked like a brick of a book.

"Hi," I said, but didn't receive an answer. "Hey," I tried again, a bit louder.

The girl looked up, then pointed at her ears. She jumped to the floor and tapped the keyboard next to a huge computer screen with a familiar fruit logo. The music died in an instant.

"Sorry. Couldn't hear you over the music," she chirped.

"It was kind of loud," I said, hoping I didn't come off as rude.

"You moving in?"

"Door number six."

"Sweet. You're right next to me. I'm Charlotte Carolina Medina Hargraves by the way, but life's too short for all that. Call me Charlie." She twitched her nose, and her glasses didn't manage to take away the glint in her dark brown eyes. "My parents never could agree on anything."

I glanced at the print on Charlie's t-shirt and almost laughed. *Don't let the Muggles bring you down* was written in large letters, decorated with a wand and sparkling stars. I had no idea what a muggle was, but it still made me smile.

"Ok, Charlie. I'm Ruby." I looked from the Captain Marvel poster above Charlie's bed to the book she had left open. "You studying already?"

"Have to stay on top of things, you know. History buff." Charlie raised her hand in the air to point at herself.

"Journalism," I said.

"Cool. We're both sort of in the research department then. Jen studies history too, but she's going to focus on women's history and cultural studies. I'm majoring in the Portuguese colonisation of Brazil. Jen and I moved in on September 9th—gosh, we've been here two weeks already, and Duncan was here before us. He's in room five, Jen's in four."

I turned the key in my hand. "You want to go with me to Freshers' Fair?" The question sort of fell out of my mouth. "Honestly, this place is huge. I had planned to go but I'm not sure where anything is."

"Sure thing. They'll be open all week, but we should get in line to make sure we get the best stuff—" Charlie glanced at her phone. "Within the next half hour. Got to get there early."

"I'll just dump my stuff and maybe take a quick shower first, if that's ok?"

"If you must. But I won't wait any longer than thirty minutes. The coupons will fly like hot cupcakes, and I want to grab as many freebies as possible."

"I'll be quick."

A green light came on as I shoved the key card into the slot by the door to my room. I pushed it open with my shoulder and dropped my backpack onto the bed before sitting next to it.

It wasn't bad. About the same size as my room back home. It had a desk, a bed and a bin, as well as a fair number of shelves. It would do. There was one other door in the room, and I sent a silent thank you to Mum, who had agreed to let me rent an en suite. It cost a bit extra, though we both valued my privacy. For a moment, I wished they had allowed pets on campus. No one had claimed Kit when I left home, not that I thought anyone would come to our cottage way outside Cheshire, and I considered him part of our little family by now. Mum had grown quite attached to the furry animal, and I was glad she had company when I wasn't around.

I fell back on the bed. A few cracks ran across the peeling paint, and several pieces of blue tack were plastered to the assumedly once white ceiling, which was more of a brownish yellow at this point. I wasn't sure why anyone would put posters up on the ceiling, though. There was enough wall space for four or five good-sized posters if I wanted to decorate the walls, but I didn't need a poster falling on my head while I was sleeping.

My joints ached and I wanted to curl up for a while, but Charlie was waiting.

Ten minutes later, I had pulled on a fresh pair of jeans and a green tank top. With no time to dry my unruly hair, I braided it to one side instead. A couple of quick strokes with mascara and I was all set.

The sound of someone knocking made me nearly poke my eye out.

"Come in," I called as I dug the mascara back into my sparsely filled make-up bag.

"Ready?"

Charlie stood in the doorway with the Instagrammer I had met earlier, Jen. She towered at least a head above Charlie, though I could swear they were both about the same age as me.

"Hey, Red," Jen said. "Later came sooner than expected, no?"

"I knew I heard a little bell at the back of my head when Charlie mentioned a Jen," I said, smiling and holding out my hand to her. "Thanks for your help earlier."

"No probs."

"You've met?" Charlie asked.

"Briefly," I said.

"But enough to know that we clicked," Jen said. "Right, Red?"

"Definitely," I said, my heart thumping with excitement.

Charlie looked at her phone and tapped the screen. "We've really got to get going. There's bound to be a line already."

Jen rolled her eyes. "Relax. There's a ton of goodies to go around. We'll be fine."

"I'm ready," I said as I shoved my phone and key card into my back pockets before exiting the room.

I was off to Freshers' Fair. What a rush. Little Ruby Morgan from Cheshire was a real student in London! I knew, deep in my heart, that whatever came next, my life was about to change.

7

Freshers' Fair looked every bit what I had read, and then some. When the three of us rounded the corner of one of the buildings, I just had to smile. This was why I needed to go to a real university. All those people, all the noise, all the possibilities!

Outside a five-storey building, Walton Hall, according to the sign above the doors, at least twenty-five tents and pavilions were spread out on the lawn. Hundreds of students buzzed between the stands, carrying canvas bags with varying logos and colours—some of them already stuffed to the brim.

"I'm prepared to break my back carrying freebies," Jen said. "And I know exactly where to start. I'm dying for a slice of pizza."

She strolled to the nearest pavilion where two women in pink waitress uniforms were handing out slices as fast as they could.

I inhaled the smell of pizza and looked at Charlie,

who wiggled her eyebrows and nodded back at me before we ran after our starving friend.

"So, now we know Franco's is an acceptable pizza place," Jen said between bites. "We need a pub as well, but we'll work that out later."

"I think I'll look for the journalist club," I said, washing down the last bite with a gulp of lemonade from Franco's logoed bottle. "They call it *The Real Truth Society*, would you believe?"

"Not the fake news, huh?" Charlie winked at me. "But yes, go find your partners in crime, Rubes. Jen and I will—"

"Please, call me Ru, ok? Rubes has a creepy ring in my ears. Long story."

"And I'm Jen as it rolls easier off your British tongues," Jen said. "So—meet up in half an hour, oui?" She looked around, using her height to its full advantage. "There!" She pointed. "That sign says meeting point."

Charlie and I agreed.

On my phone, the uni app told me that the journalists' stand was inside. I looked at Jen and Charlie, who had already moved to the next stand, grabbing a canvas bag each to start filling them with freebies. Charlie grinned at me, and I smiled back. Two friends already. That should put a smile on my mum's face too, when I texted her later.

I looked down on my phone again and didn't notice the shadow coming at me from the right. The collision would have sent me flying had it not been for the shadow grabbing my arm. It pulled me up inches before I hit the old stone steps leading into Walton Hall.

"Whoa!" said the shadow. "You ok?"

I turned my head from the worn-out steps to a smiling face. A dark shadow of stubble framed the smile, and the stranger's eyes looked at me, worried. Eyes that made me reconsider renaming my own blue eyes to a lesser version of the colour.

"Y-yes, thank you," I said, steadying myself. "I'm sorry, I wasn't paying attention."

"No, please," said the blue-eyed stubble guy. "It was my fault entirely. Stupid to run around with all these people here. Name's Brendan, by the way, Brendan O'Callaghan."

The Irish accent nearly made my knees buckle again but his grip held me firmly in place. He let go of my arm and held his hand out to greet me.

I shook it. "Ruby. Ruby Morgan."

"So, Ruby Ruby Morgan, where are you headed?"

That smile. I swallowed and hoped he didn't notice. *Get a grip, girl.*

"To the—eh—" Crap, where was I going again? "Journalist stand," I finally managed.

"Cool, that's just next to my society. Allow me, Lady Lady Morgan?"

"Just Ruby, please. And thanks, but I'll manage without the support."

To be honest, I felt more than a little compelled to link my arm into his as if we were walking into this old building at a different day in time, when it was shiny and new. I had no intention of any romantic activities, though. Studying would require all my time, and I also needed to find a job if I was to have any hope of affording to stay at uni.

Inside, Brendan strolled through the corridor and into what I assumed was the actual Walton Hall. The double doors were open, and the hall was just as full of students and noise as the area outside, if not more.

I followed Brendan as he manoeuvred through the crowd, zigging and zagging when he did, eventually finding myself in front of a table with a wide-eyed girl behind it. The sign above her said *The Real Truth Society*.

"Here we are, milady," said Brendan, taking a dramatic bow.

The gesture was both a little cute and a little funny. I almost made a curtsy, feigning holding my skirt up to the sides, but thought the better of it. "Thank you again, Brendan. Very gentleman-like of you."

"I'm right over here." He nodded at the next stand over. "Come and say hello when you're done selling your soul to the truth, yeah?"

I let out a little laugh.

"Hi, honey!" said the girl behind the table, her American heritage apparent through three syllables.

"Hello. I'm taking a Journalism BA, and understand this is the right club to join?"

"The only one, baby!" said the American girl and turned the iPad on the table towards me. "Just enter your student ID there, and your soul is apparently ours." She said the last words loudly enough for Brendan to hear.

He snapped his fingers. "I knew it!" he called. "Don't do it, Ruby Ruby! Please, stay with us mortals!" He let his voice drift away, kneeling and stretching his arms towards me at the same time.

"Jeez," the girl moaned. "If I wanted to hear an

Irishman complaining, I'd go to a U2 concert and hear Bono cry about the environment or something."

I stifled a giggle and entered the last digits of my ID, then watched as my name and profile picture popped up on the screen. "Is this you?" it said in a box underneath. I tapped the "Yes" button, and made a mental note to change the picture—if that was an option. The girl that had snapped the selfie two weeks earlier, when she registered in the student admin system, had been both afraid and excited. It showed. I wanted to leave the old Cheshire Ruby behind, and look more confident and grown up.

"Diane Cooper," the American girl said, and looked at the iPad. "Welcome, Ruby Morgan!"

"Thanks. Do I do anything now, or—?"

"We're desperately in need of more people on the stand," Diane said. "If you want, you could help out here during the week?"

"Sure. Tomorrow, maybe?"

"Or Thursday—totally up to you. But yeah, that'd be great. Also, we're having a party tonight." She handed me a flyer. "It's not mandatory, but trust me, you don't wanna miss it." She winked and turned her attention to a boy who had come to the table. "Hi there!"

I looked at the neighbouring stand, but Brendan was busy helping a couple of students filling their bags. I turned and walked outside again. Maybe I should get one of those bags myself, and see if Jen's freebie talk was worth it? I still had another fifteen minutes until I was to meet—

"—the fudge is your problem?" a girl shouted nearby.

Didn't I know that voice? I found my way back outside and searched for the source.

It *was* Charlie. She was standing toe to toe with a girl behind a pavilion at the edge of the fair. The other girl had her finger up in Charlie's face, and they were seconds away from throwing punches. The familiar tingling in my blood began as small balls of light formed in my palms. I started towards the girls, trying not to run.

"You just stay away, slag!" said the other girl.

Her short black hair made me think of that punk rock woman. What was her name? One of Dad's old vinyl album covers flashed before my eyes.

"I've had enough of you edging in on my man!"

"Your man?" Charlie spat the words out with a laugh. "If he is your *man*," she drew air quotes with her fingers, "then he really shouldn't come on to me like that."

The punk girl closed her fist and aimed for Charlie.

I didn't stop to think. In an instant, I had sent a magic push through the air. The force field was small, just enough to encapsulate Charlie's head, but it did the job. Punkie's hand hit the field, snapping Charlie's head backwards. To the hitter, it would hopefully appear as though she had landed the punch, though it would do no damage at all to Charlie, thanks to my force field.

I had closed in on the girls and was just eight or ten steps away. Charlie looked puzzled, which gave the punk girl enough time to throw a second punch. Or rather, a kick. Her black boot hit Charlie in the kneecap. I couldn't react fast enough.

"Ouch!" Charlie screamed, and lunged at the other girl, toppling the both of them to the ground.

I withdrew the force field as I came up to the fighters and grabbed Charlie by the shoulders. From the corner of my eye, I noticed a few people had gathered around us. With all my strength, I managed to pull my friend off —Siouxsie Sioux! *That* was the name of the punk rocker. For a split second, I could hear Dad telling me to pronounce it "Suzy Su" before my mind returned to the brawl.

"Let go!" Charlie shouted, trying to wiggle out of my grip.

The girl on the ground was halfway up on her knees, getting ready to throw herself, and her fists—or worse, her boots again—at Charlie. I couldn't use any more magic. Too many people; some were bound to see the nearly invisible force field if I used it.

"Right, that's enough," rumbled a voice. A man came forward, splitting the crowd like Moses and the Red Sea with an elaborate cane in his hand. He looked like he had come straight out of an 18th-century colonial film, with his long stylish coat and black buckled shoes. "This is not how we celebrate Freshers' Week, ladies. Come on!"

He grabbed the punk girl and helped her to her feet while still holding her flailing arms away from Charlie. Charlie backed up a couple of steps, but only because I dragged her that way.

"We're not done, bitch," the punk girl yelled, waving two fingers in the air towards Charlie.

"Piss off. Go take care of your *man*, dimwit," Charlie

retorted, turning the air quote fingers into the same obscene gesture.

The crowd parted just as quickly as it had assembled when the fight was over, and I heard a couple of boys complain as we walked past. "Not much of a fight," one of them said, the other laughing in response.

"What the hell, Charlie?" Jen sat her already stuffed canvas bag on the ground, letting out a groan of relief.

Charlie just pulled a whatever face and shrugged. "Just an insecure tosser not being able to keep her bull in tow. Well, not really a bull, more a donkey to be honest. He hit on me at a party last night, and I guess the news reached her."

She turned to me, squinting her eyes for a second. "Thanks, I guess. Although I'm pretty sure I'd have taken her." She tilted her head ever so slightly and beamed at me. "Her jab was weak. Like butterfly kiss kind of weak."

I held my breath.

Charlie winked and gave herself a mock punch on the chin. "Guess it pays to have had your face punched a lot. It is bound to harden even the softest of baby cheeks eventually."

I wasn't sure why Charlie would have had her face punched before, but I didn't press. As the three of us restarted the quest for more vouchers, USB-sticks, mugs and whatever valuables to fill our bags with, I felt a knot tighten in my stomach. I was such a muppet.

Charlie knew!

8

I sat cross-legged on Charlie's bed, twisting my fingers. The girl rummaged through her wardrobe, chucking t-shirts and jeans on the floor.

"What are you wearing tonight?" she asked, her voice muffled as she spoke into the almost empty shelf where her head was.

"I figured I could just wear what I'm wearing now." I had not spent a second worrying about what clothes to wear. I had, however, spent the last few hours turning the day's events in my head. I could almost hear my mum yelling at me, picture her coming to London to drag my ass back to Cheshire. And uni hadn't even started yet. How dumb could I get?

Jen strode into the room and propped herself next to me. "Nope. You're not wearing the same thing you wore all day. You know there will be boys at the party, right? And you really need to wear your hair down. I think I might have exactly the thing for you. I need to change too, so I'll find it for you. Back in a beat."

She bounced back up and disappeared into the hallway. The sound of her door shutting behind her left a heavy silence in the room.

"Charlie," I said.

"Ru," Charlie said, extending the sound of the u for an extra second.

"Can we talk?"

Charlie leaned out of the wardrobe, turning to me. "Sure you're ready? You know, we don't have to."

"I need to know you're good with this." I gestured at myself and Charlie stood to close the door.

She pulled out the chair by her desk, straddling it the wrong way around, and folded her arms on the back of it. "I do have questions, but only if you're ready."

This was probably a worse idea than using my magic in the first place. Perhaps I should have tried convincing Charlie that it was all in her head, but that would be a mean thing to do. Even though I was reluctant, there was a part of me that wanted to tell Charlie everything. I had been hiding for so long it might be good to tell the truth for once. Stupid or not.

"Shoot," I said.

Charlie rested her chin on her arms. "What was that you did to me earlier? Was that a force field? Is that your power, I mean, or can you do more? I've never met a Mag in person before. Not that I know of anyway."

I sucked in a breath and my body tensed. I didn't know where to begin to explain. What would happen if Charlie told on me? We had only just met. Could I trust her to keep a secret like this? Did I have a choice?

"That's a lot of questions with longer answers, but

yes, that was a force field. But Charlie, you can't tell anyone."

"I think it's cool."

"I don't. It's just a part of who I am that no one else can know about. Promise me. Please!"

Charlie lowered her forehead, looking at me over the rim of her glasses.

"If it's that important to you, I won't. It seems tiring, though, always hiding what you are. And if you don't mind, what exactly are you?"

I hesitated. The cat was out of the bag, however, so I might as well let it stay there. "Fae," I whispered.

"Fae? As in, you're a fairy?" Her head popped up and the corners of her mouth drew wide.

I nodded.

"That's awesome! I didn't know there were Fae. Sorcerers and Shifters I know about, but Fae?" She wiggled her eyebrows. "Do you have wings under that top?"

I giggled. It wasn't as absurd as Charlie clearly thought it was. I didn't have wings, but I would have if I had been born on Avalon—or so I imagined anyway.

"Nope. No wings, I'm afraid. I'm pretty much like you, with a bit of magic attached."

Charlie extended her hand. I returned the gesture and she wrapped her pinkie around mine. "I swear not to tell a living soul."

I exhaled with relief as the door swung open again, and a lanky boy stumbled into the room.

"Ready to get your boots on?" Dark circles framed his brown eyes and he didn't look like he had washed for a week. His jeans were tattered, and the faded, once-black Led Zeppelin t-shirt had definitely seen better days.

"Dunc," Charlie said, narrowing her gaze at him.

"Char," he replied with a sharp edge of sarcasm.

"This is Ruby, our new flatmate. Ruby, this is Duncan. Remember I told you about our fourth flatmate?"

"Cool, another girl." Duncan grinned.

Charlie shook her head at Duncan. "You look like shit, Dunc. Maybe you should sit this one out?"

"Nuh-uh. I have a date tonight." He scratched his neck and continued to wipe his eyes with the heels of his hands.

"With a girl?"

"Let's call her Harvey." He smirked. "It's really more of an exchange than a date. You up for it? I can ask for a couple extra."

Charlie shifted her head back and forth between Duncan and me. "Nah, not tonight. I'm good, thanks."

"Let me know if you change your mind. My supplier says she's got a fresh untainted batch. Don't want to miss out." He ruffled Charlie's hair and wobbled back outside.

I gawked at my new friend, not able to keep my mouth closed. Not her too. Was everyone on MagX these days?

Charlie averted her gaze. "Don't look at me like that. I've only done it a few times. Always at a party, and never more than a tiny drop."

"Are you insane?"

I sucked my lips between my teeth. I had to stay calm. The fire burning in my veins didn't agree with me, however. I wanted to slap Charlie for her sheer idiocy when a small flame ignited in my palm. Gasping, I slapped myself instead and the flame disappeared. What was I doing? And what was that feeling of my veins catching fire? I stood, shaking, then rushed into Charlie's bathroom and splashed water on my face.

My mascara ran in black rivers over my cheeks but at least I was cooling off. This was new. I had never done anything like that before. It didn't feel right. Although, a fire power was kind of awesome, if I could control it. *Crap.* This was not the best time to learn how to control a new power. If that was even what this was. Mum had never said anything about the Fae having fire powers.

"You all right in there?" Charlie called.

I stepped back into the room. "Got some cleaning wipes?"

"Sure." It took Charlie a few seconds to grab the wipes and hand them to me.

I started cleaning my face. "MagX isn't fun," I mumbled.

"How would you know? You've got magic all the time. Is it so wrong of me to want to feel like a better version of myself? MagX makes me feel. Alive."

We sat quietly for a long time. How could I convince her to stop taking something that gave her these amazing feelings? There was only one argument that came to mind, one I did not share lightly.

"Sit with me?" I gestured at the bed and we sat opposite each other. I took Charlie's hands.

"You won't burn me?" Charlie asked.

"You saw that?"

"It was a bit scary," Charlie said. "And fudging awesome."

"Well, I would never burn you." Would I, though? "Not on purpose, at least."

"I think I'll keep my hands to myself then," she said, letting go of mine.

Though I understood, it still felt like a stab to my heart. Charlie was scared of me.

"Listen." I had to start somewhere. "What just happened has never happened before. I didn't know I had this in me. But that's not why I got angry, or why I cried." I curled the sheets in my hands. "My dad. He died seven years ago."

She gasped. "I'm so sorry to hear that."

"It still hurts like hell. But here's my point. He died after he OD'd on MagX. I don't know how it happened but sometimes the blood doesn't agree with a human host. I've been tracking incidents ever since I started interning at my local newspaper. We're talking about advanced chemistry to get the blood from a Mag to become MagX."

"Yeah, something about reducing the number of blue blood cells, right?"

Although that was a simplification, I nodded. "The ratio between our blue cells and the human red and white ones, yes. Problem is, not all dealers can get their hands on clean MagX, or they do the separation and mixing themselves. The blood is often diluted—or worse, tainted—and when it is, it's deadly. I don't want anyone else to die from this. Especially not you."

Another long pause followed before Charlie folded her hands in mine, making my shoulders relax. "I get it.

You have to understand, though. Magic, to a human, is intoxicating. The thrill of it is unlike anything any human can ever hope to experience in their lifetime, a sense of godliness. People are not going to stop taking MagX because of some random cases of people dying. There are a bunch of other reasons why that might happen to someone."

"I just—I want it gone," I said. "The revelation of magical beings in the world was supposed to make it easier. We were supposed to be able to be who we are. Instead, everyone still has to hide. And to top it all off, there are people harvesting our blood so that others can have a moment of—what did you call it? Godliness."

Charlie pushed her glasses up the ridge of her nose. "You're pretty but I wouldn't peg you for a goddess." She gave me a half-smile.

The door opened again and Jen pranced back inside. Her hair was down, and she had changed into a tight navy-blue one-piece with no bra on, and a cleavage so deep it was a surprise her belly button wasn't showing.

"Here," said Jen, sending a top through the air to land on my head. "Wear this." She went to sit on the windowsill, staring at me as I tried to figure out which way the top was meant to be worn. "Oh, poppet, your face. You'll need an entire makeover. Lucky for you, I'm an expert."

I didn't have it in me to argue. Part of me wanted to skip the entire night and roll into bed, but I wanted to keep an eye on Charlie to make sure she didn't get in any trouble. Or take anything she wasn't supposed to.

"I'm all yours, Jen," I said with as much enthusiasm as I could muster.

Jen clapped her hands and retrieved her make-up bag. It was three times the size of the one I had in my room. I didn't know what half the stuff inside was even for, but surrendered to the so-called expert. It took a full half-hour before Jen was satisfied with her creation.

"Now, lose the braid and let me see that hair."

I did as I was told. As predicted, my hair fell in thick waves around my shoulders, and Jen smirked.

"No need to do anything with that gorgeous mane. You'll have boys falling left, right and centre just from that."

Boys? I wasn't going out to meet boys. Although there was an Irish bloke I wouldn't mind seeing.

"Hey, you with us?"

Charlie and Jen stood in the doorway and I got to my feet.

"Sure am."

Jen held her phone up. "Get in here. Give me your best strong woman face."

With no idea what kind of face that would be, I gave her my best fake smile.

Jen took a bunch of pictures before she pocketed her phone.

"*Hashtag Feminism*," she said before we all strolled outside like Charlie's Angels on a mission. "First stop, the Old Willow. That's going to be our pub."

9

INTENSE CHATTER AND LOUD BANTER SOUNDED FROM THE pub, making my head spin already. I had never been comfortable with large crowds. There was a slight autumn chill in the air and we decided—that is, Jen decided—to find a table inside. I regretted it the moment I laid eyes on the busy throng of people. There was hardly any air left to breathe. It didn't help much that people were smoking inside, even though there was a ban on smoking in public places.

Jen turned her head from the bar stretching across the back wall to the clusters of round tables. "There. Someone is leaving." She linked her arms with Charlie and me, rushing us forward. As we neared the table, she sped up, let go of our arms and all but lunged into the nearest chair.

Another group of girls gawked at her and received a lopsided grin from Jen in response. "Sorry. Got to move your feet next time. This table is taken." She turned to Charlie and me as the other group strutted off. "Sit."

"I think I'll go get us some drinks," Charlie said. "Three Coronas all right?"

We nodded and Charlie shimmied off to the bar.

Two large screens on either side of the counter were on, and most of the boys had their eyes glued to the football match. I smiled as I recognised the red colours of the home team. Dad's team. No—our team! I wrinkled my nose at the white shirts and blue shorts of the opposing players, in the way I remembered Dad would whenever United walked out on Anfield. I rarely watched Liverpool play anymore. It hurt too much, but maybe that part was getting easier at last, as I found myself cheering along when Firmino put the ball between the legs of the goalie and into the net.

"You like football?" Jen asked.

"Used to watch it all the time with my dad," I said.

"Huh. Would not have guessed. I honestly don't understand the fuss." She raised an eyebrow as Roberto Firmino pulled up his shirt, sliding forwards on the grass on his knees. "Although, it sure has its moments."

He would get a booking for that one, I thought.

The channel changed, and a woman news anchor filled the screen.

"Get off!" someone yelled. "Who has the remote?"

It was too loud to hear what the anchor said but a blue text banner, which ran across the bottom of the image, delivered the message clearly enough. There had been a robbery at Tiffany's in Old Bond Street. A series of images of empty shelves and two cashiers being treated by medics followed. The robbers had taken everything. I sighed heavily as I read on. One of the robbers wasn't human and had used his magic to compel the staff to do everything he asked. What a tosser. Like it wasn't hard enough for Mags as it was.

A bottle crashed to the floor and a group of guys started whistling. And there he was. Brendan. He sat two tables apart from me with a group of boys. His eyes were exactly as I remembered, and a slight tingle rose in my chest.

Charlie returned as one of the boys slammed his fist on the table.

"Bloody freaks. Get them off our streets! And put the game back on," the boy shouted.

"They sure taste great, though," another one said before they bumped fists and burst out laughing.

Charlie gave me a look while pushing a bottle toward me, the obligatory lime stuffed into the neck of it. "Here. Hold this. It's really cold."

I grimaced at her but grabbed the bottle. Message received. This would be a dangerous place to have fire shoot from my hands.

"Good call," I whispered.

"*Hashtag Racism,*" Jen announced and snapped a picture of the boys before she stood and waltzed over to Brendan's table. "You're a bunch of rotting racists," she said with as loud a voice as possible without yelling.

"Chill, babe." The boy who had called out freaks leaned back in his chair, eyeing Jen up and down. His shoulders were broad, his light brown hair ruffled with intent to just the right amount of dishevelled.

"Chill?" Jen lifted one side of her lip in blatant disgust.

He winked at her and reached out. I wasn't sure what he was planning to do, but was relieved when

Brendan's hand wrapped around his friend's arm, firmly moving it backwards.

"Behave," Brendan said, then turned to Jen. "He's had one too many tonight. We would be very happy if you would join us, though. If he gets bothersome, we'll kick his arse back to his room." He was still talking to Jen, but his gaze had turned to me.

I stared back at him, unable to avert my eyes, before he broke the connection and smiled at Jen. "So, what do you say?"

Jen crossed her arms, tapping her left foot against the floor. "I'll have to check with my girls first. Not sure why they would want to sit with a narrow-minded bunch like you lot. Unless you decide to kick that one—" She angled her head at the drunken friend. "To the curb."

"I'm sorry, all right? Game's back on, so can we just leave it?" the boy mumbled. "Why are babes always so sensitive?"

"People are people," Jen said. "Not freaks. I'm not *babes* to you, and our streets are everyone's streets. This is 2019, dumbass. Or are you the kind that would rather close the borders and have me sit at home, knitting socks?"

"People are people, sure. Mags, however, are not." The boy tripped on his words, blinking fast as if he had something stuck in his eye. "They don't belong here."

"And where do you suppose they should go?" Jen held her arms together so tight, her veins looked like they were about to pop out of her skin. She was probably fighting the urge to slap him as much as I was straining not to set fire to anything.

I clutched the bottle tightly in my hands, taking deep breaths. Not here.

The boy opened his mouth, then shut it. His body convulsed before he scrambled out of his seat and stumbled outside as fast as his brawny legs could carry him.

Brendan shrugged, then waved at me. "You wanna join us? Nick's out for the rest of the night."

Charlie handed me her drink and picked up two chairs, nodding at the boys. As we neared the table, Brendan pulled out Nick's now empty chair, inviting me to sit.

"Hello again, Ruby Ruby Morgan," he said.

"Hey." The word stuck in my throat and came out a pitch higher than intended. He remembered my name.

"Sorry about the mess. Nick is better served sober."

"Somehow I doubt that," I said.

Brendan smirked and I picked the lime from my drink, squeezing a few drops into the bottle.

"So, you're Irish, huh?" I almost pounded my head on the table. What a stupid thing to ask. Like I couldn't think of anything better to say? Of course he was Irish. Great job. He had to think I was hiding a head of blonde tresses underneath all that red.

"Sure looks like it."

I grabbed at the first common denominator that sprang to mind. "You know Diane?"

"Only since Monday. Word is she and her crew throws a mean party, though." He glanced at his phone. "Speaking of which, the pub is about to close. You girls going to Diane's?"

Charlie downed the last swig of her Corona before

placing the bottle firmly on the table. "Of course we are."

We left as a group, having added Brendan and three of his mates to our entourage for the night. Charlie was chatting up a bloke named John, while Jen had two boys, Jack and Reece, one on each arm, leading the way.

Brendan and I trailed a few paces behind the others. We didn't talk much, but it wasn't that awkward silence you sometimes get when you're around strangers and don't know exactly what to say. It just *was*.

An almost full moon shone down on us, and the sky was lit with stars reflected on the still water of the lake. We were walking underneath an archway of lilacs when Brendan bumped my shoulder, angling his head at Charlie and his friend.

"John doesn't stand a chance, does he?"

I exhaled in a puff. "Probably not."

"That's what I thought."

An old building rose ahead. It was beautifully maintained, no peeling paint, and the arched windows looked like they had been set in place only yesterday.

A girl stumbled past us as John opened the door to Raven Court for Charlie. The booming notes from 'Higher Love' thundered from the large speakers on either side of the room. Jen was escorted by Jack and Reece, while Brendan and I walked in last.

"Jello shot?" A lanky boy with spiky black hair and skin the colour of a late autumn sunset presented us with a tray full of small cups ranging in colours from yellow to deep purple.

"Don't mind if I do," Jen said, leaning forwards. "We'll all take one."

I hesitated but Jen placed a cup of red jello firmly in my hand and gave me a stern look.

"Cheers," Brendan said.

Everyone cheered back and the cups were all empty seconds later. I looked around the group, all staring back at me as I still had a full cup in my hand.

"Oh, sod off," I said, then downed the jello in one go. It really tasted like jello and not like whatever else was bound to be in the mix.

The boy with the tray swayed on his feet. "Awesome. Welcome to Raven Court. There's punch in the kitchen. And more shots." He winked and scurried off.

"Punch!" Charlie grabbed John's arm and walked straight into Duncan.

"Hey, Char," Duncan snorted. "Fun night, huh? Meet Liv."

Liv was half standing, half supporting herself on Duncan and the nearest table. Her knees were bent at odd angles and she had streaks of mascara underneath her eyes, mirroring her clotted lashes. She glanced at me and the others, then turned her head up at Duncan.

"I need—" she started but never finished. Her mouth opened and closed as if she was trying to trap flies with it.

"Sorry girls." Duncan snickered. "We have a date." The two of them hobbled past our group and into the night.

Charlie stared at the closed door for a moment before she grabbed onto John's arm again. "Punch, right?"

The boy grinned at her and nodded before they strutted off.

Jen poked the boys at her sides on the shoulders. "We

don't need any punch. I've got my own stash." She opened her navy-blue bag, a perfect match for her one-piece, showing everyone the bottles inside. "Catch you later," she said and walked off with the boys.

"That leaves us then, Ruby Rubes," Brendan said.

"Please don't call me Rubes," I said, holding my hand up apologetically. "Don't ask."

"As long as you stick to B, and not Bren, we're good." He smacked his lips. "B B works, too. Or the even better O'Callaghan O'Callaghan."

I laughed. "Yeah, 'cause that wasn't long-winded at all."

A couple got up from a sofa further into the room and I took Brendan's hand, pulling him with me before I had a chance to think about it. I retracted my arm and we dumped down on the soft velvet pillows. Raven Court was much more spacious than our flat. The living room alone was probably four times the size of the one we had at Craydon.

"How many people live here?" I asked.

"Diane, and three others. This is the poshest place on campus. You can bet your shorts her parents have deep pockets."

It did look expensive. Especially for student housing. "That reminds me, I need to start looking for a job."

Brendan lit up. "Milady." He stared at me with those sparkly blue eyes again. "Your knight is at your service. I happen to know a place looking for people right now. Nick works there, so you've already got an in."

"And where might this magical job be, oh knight." I bit my lip. I had decided to play along but it turned out sounding exactly as cheesy as I was hoping to avoid.

Brendan didn't seem to mind, however, and he took my hand again. It was warm to the touch, his skin rougher than I would have expected. I hadn't taken the time to notice the feel of his hand when I mindlessly guided him to the first free seat I could find.

"It's at a cinema down in Croydon," he said. "Pay's below decent but it's a paying job for doing next to nothing. Plus, they give you free film posters." He inched closer. "I'll make sure Nick gets you an interview. It's just a formality, though. That place will hire anybody, so the job is practically yours already if you want it."

"Oh, anybody, you say? Even me?"

"I didn't mean it like—"

"Relax, B. I'm just having a laugh. I really do want a job, and appreciate your help."

Did I want a job, though? My mum had been very clear I needed one. Wanting one, however, was not the same. But this sounded like an easy solution.

"Settled then. I'll talk to Nick when he's sober," Brendan said and pulled his fingers through his thick hair, wiggling to fall deeper into the sofa, making me sink further down as well. I was about to open my mouth to say something stupid again when Charlie sauntered over with a girl on her arm.

"What happened to John?" I asked.

"He was chugging down a jug of beer last I saw." Charlie chuckled, snuggling closer to the girl. "Oh, this is … Emma?" She looked at the girl like a big question mark was painted on her forehead.

"It's Helen!" Helen tossed her hair back and stomped off to the makeshift dance floor where she started dancing with another girl.

"Oops," Charlie said, her eyes shifting to the door and back again. "Seems I lost another one tonight. I think I'll sniff around a bit more, though."

She walked off again, but I didn't take my eyes off my friend. It was more than obvious where Charlie was headed, even if she was slipping in and out of clusters of people, taking large detours to her final destination—the door. I frowned as Charlie eased her way outside.

I stood, Brendan's hand dropping out of mine.

"I need to check on her. I think."

"Why? Seems like she can handle herself."

"She has this habit I'm not sure she can shake."

He raised his eyebrows like he understood exactly what I meant. "Sounds like you better go find her then." He bounced out of the sofa. "See you around Ruby Ruby Morgan."

And then he was off. I hadn't had time to blink before he was getting his groove on next to Emma. Or was it Helen? That had taken a quick turn, but I didn't have time to be insulted. I all but ran for the door, nearly tripping over Duncan's date on the steps outside.

Liv gave me an annoyed look before she crawled past the steps and curled up by the wall. We would have to check on her later. No one should be alone in a state like that. Right now, however, I had to find Charlie.

My gut was churning, telling me that I had more than a little reason for concern. It was my inherited intuition, Mum used to say, the fact that I could sense things others couldn't. It was often hard to separate the feelings I got from my normal paranoia, but Mum had repeatedly tried to teach me to trust my instincts, and this was one time when I would.

I passed a few people as I hurried through the archway of lilacs near Raven Court and onto the large area of green surrounding the lake.

A shadow moved behind a tree and the sight of it made my skin prickle. It reminded me of something from a dream—my childhood maybe? What was that? It was too quick for me to get a real look at it, and yet it was like something awful had seeped into my skin. The undeniable feeling of dread grew with every breath as I moved closer before running down to where the shadow had been. It was the same tree where I had seen the girl in red sneakers at my arrival.

A short laugh issued from behind the trunk. Charlie's laugh.

"There you are." I drew in a deep breath, steadying myself.

"It's amazeballs, Ru. You've got to try this." Charlie levitated a hair's breadth off the ground, spread her arms and floated forward on her stomach. "It makes you fly."

"Charlie!"

"Oh, right. You don't need this, do you?" She twirled mid-air, shifting her body to face me. "Fly with me."

"I can't fly." I crossed my arms.

"Sure about that? You're missing out big time." She laughed again, louder and more intensely this time.

I dropped to my bottom with the trunk at my back, glaring at Charlie. Had we not had this conversation only hours ago? Granted, we didn't know each other that well yet, but I had hoped to make Charlie understand. My roommate belted out some song I didn't recognise before she twirled a few times more above the lake and back again. The song stopped suddenly, and Charlie's hands flew to her chest. She plummeted to the ground like a rock being dropped off a cliff.

"Charlie?" I knelt next to her.

There was no response. Charlie kept clutching her chest and her body jittered. Her eyes rolled back, leaving only a tiny slit of white between her eyelids.

"Charlie. Don't joke about this!"

I was grasping. This was evidently no joke. My new friend was having a heart attack. Like Dad. Only then, I hadn't been there to help him. I sniffled and shook my head. I was here now.

"I won't let you die!"

I turned my head back, but nothing seemed to move apart from a few leaves in the wind, so I continued to drag Charlie into the shade of the tree. One day. One single day, and I was already as far out of the safe zone as I could get. Maybe Mum had been right. Coming here had been a risk, and I had not cared to consider how big a risk it was.

"You owe me big time," I said before twisting Charlie's hands apart and putting my own down over her heart. The warm sensation of my magic sparked up in my veins like it had so many times before, coursing through my blood to expel from my skin, at the same time expelling the earlier sensation of dread along with it. A glow like a small sun formed in my palms, rays of golden hues twisting over Charlie's torso. If anyone was watching, they would already know what I was, but I couldn't think about that now. I had to save my friend.

"Come on, hun," I whispered.

Charlie's heartbeat was slow. Too slow. Why wasn't it

working?

"Come on," I cried. It had to work but Charlie was almost gone already. "Don't you dare die on me like this. You hear me, Charlie? Fight!"

The heartbeats were almost gone, beating further and further apart. Drops of perspiration trickled down my temples when the pounding beneath my palms began to speed up again. Closer now. Harder. Spots of red blended with the sun-like colours before Charlie's eyes flew open.

She coughed and rolled to her side, shivering as if it were midwinter.

"You're all right," I said, wiping my face and drawing the cool air into my lungs. "You're all right!" I removed my jacket, placed it over my friend, and watched as the magic retracted back into my body.

Someone moved through the archway, and a familiar voice called out.

"Ruby? Charlie?" Jen turned towards us and sprinted to the tree. "What the hell happened?"

"She got some tainted blood, I think. Nearly lost her."

"*Merde!* Stupid girl."

We wrapped our arms around Charlie, supporting her as best we could.

"We need to get her to the hospital," Jen said.

"No," I said, a little too snappy.

Jen tilted her head, her brows low.

"I mean, MagX is illegal," I continued. "And she's better now than she was. She would kill us if we messed up her education."

"True. We'll take her back to Craydon then. But first

sign that she's not recovering, I'll take her to the hospital."

"Deal."

With some effort, we got Charlie home and into bed. We covered her in duvets, and her skin slowly began to regain some colour. I had healed her heart, but even I couldn't clean the alcohol from her blood. She would have to sleep it off.

I was staring at the mascara under Charlie's eyes when I remembered something. "Will you watch her, Jen? I have to go back and check on someone."

"I won't leave her side," Jen said, not taking her eyes off our friend.

Charlie couldn't possibly have a better watchdog, so I left and rushed back to Raven Court. I stopped outside, scanning the area. No Liv.

"You seen Olivia? I've looked everywhere for her," someone said behind me.

I jumped as Duncan placed his arm over my shoulder.

"She was here about an hour ago," I said.

"Selfish broad. She had my last fix." He went to sit on the steps.

"She didn't look like she could go anywhere."

"Where there's a will and all that," Duncan said, and lit a cigarette.

Maybe he was right, but Liv had been in no condition to move much. I shouldn't have left her on her own. Then again, Charlie would be dead if I hadn't.

Someone had to have got her home. I decided to believe she had found help, and yet I couldn't shake the blaring bells ringing at the back of my head.

10

"RUBY?" CHARLIE'S VOICE WAS DISTANT BUT THE ALARM IN her tone made me force my eyes open.

"Yes, Charlie."

"Am I ... are we ... what happened?"

I rubbed the sleep from my eyes and sat on the arrangement of pillows on the floor by her bed. Jen was snoring, hugging the duvet, her body plastered to the wall on the other side of Charlie.

The memories of the night before flooded my mind and I choked back a sob. "You almost had a heart attack, that's what happened."

"I—" Charlie started.

"You." I shook my head at her. "You could have died. You *were* dying. Don't you get it?"

"I'm sorry. Dunc vouched for the dealer. It should have been perfectly safe."

"It's MagX. That shit is never safe. You don't know the first thing about how it was treated before it ended up on your tongue."

I was wide awake now and the worry I had felt the night before was quickly turning to anger. Charlie should have known better. The warm sensation of fire ignited in my veins and I pressed my hands into fists. What *was* that? Every time I got upset, the fire started up again. I had to learn to control it, but how? As far as I knew, fire wasn't a normal Fae power, and I didn't want to tell Mum either. She had stepped far out of her comfort zone just by letting me come to London in the first place. Nothing good would come from telling her about this.

A tear swam down Charlie's cheek. "I'm so sorry, Ru. I never realised."

"I did try to tell you, didn't I?"

"You did, and you have my word that I will listen to you in the future."

I shook, the warmth spread out, and it was as if I were sat in a sauna when the sweat began trickling from my pores. *Stop it, Ruby!* I yelled in my mind.

The touch from Charlie's hand on my shoulder made me wince. I locked eyes with her—seeing what? Concern? Regret? Whatever it was, it made me relax. I took a few deep breaths. The warmth eventually subsided and I returned to my usual body temperature.

So, I could control it—at least to an extent. Maybe all I needed was practice.

The door sprang open and Duncan's knees buckled before he hurled himself at the pillows beside me.

"Liv here?"

"Why would she be here?" Charlie asked, pulling her fingers through her dark hair, failing miserably to clear out the knots that had gathered since we left for the party the night before.

"She's vanished." Dunc licked his chapped lips.

"You did check her room before you came storming in here, right?" Charlie asked.

He stuck his tongue out. "I'm not an idiot, Char."

Vanished? Liv still hadn't shown up? A knot formed in my stomach. But why? Surely there had to be some natural explanation for Liv's disappearance, so why did my intuition scream at me that something was wrong?

"She probably hooked up with her dealer or some other loser," Charlie quipped, much more chipper than mere seconds ago.

"Nah, she don't do blood. Booze is more her thing." Dunc scratched his thighs, his pupils nearly extinguishing the brown in his eyes.

"You sure? Perhaps she traded for some MagX. She looked more than a little desperate last I saw her." Jen had rolled over to face us and was now leaning her body past Charlie's feet.

Duncan glared at her. "I'm telling you, that's not Liv. She's never touched MagX."

I somehow believed Duncan. The concern in his voice was genuine enough, but moreover, I couldn't shake the feeling rooted in my chest.

"Whatever," Jen said. She slid out of bed and stood. "Glad to see you're feeling better, Charlie. But girl, you had us scared shitless. Don't you ever do that again or I will smack you senseless myself!"

Charlie shook her head vehemently, immediately holding her hands to her temples. "Too soon," she moaned.

Jen raised her chin. "Good. That you won't do it again, I mean, not the headache. Now, I smell like a drenched cub, so I'll be in the shower for the next hour or so." She spun on her heels and left.

While I was happy that Charlie was feeling better, I couldn't make my gut unwind. My intuition had sent me down the wrong path more than once, but it had been right last night. Charlie was in trouble and I had sensed it. That same feeling was twisting around in my body about Liv, and I had to trust that it meant something.

"I believe you, Dunc," I blurted.

He gave me a lopsided smile. "Are you pulling my leg?"

"I mean it. I believe you. Liv was in no condition to go anywhere with anyone. If someone helped her, she should be in her room."

"Guess that's settled." Charlie smelled her armpits and wrinkled her nose. "I'll jump in the shower as well, though I'll only be like five minutes. Then we'll help you look for Liv. All right?"

Duncan gave us a series of quick nods like a toddler expecting treats.

I stood and rolled my duvet into a ball in my arms. "Let's all meet up in the living room in fifteen?" No way was I able to use five minutes to get ready but fifteen would be enough to look slightly decent.

After a quick shower and a freshly painted face, the painting consisting of a few strokes of mascara and lip gloss, I stood in the living room with Duncan and Charlie.

"Do we wait for Jen?" I asked.

"She'll catch up," Charlie replied. "Where to first?"

I wasn't sure. If Duncan had already been out looking, then where would be the sensible place to start? I didn't even know where the girl lived, much less where her favourite hang-out spots were.

Charlie pushed her glasses up the ridge of her nose. "We should probably alert campus security."

"No!" Duncan shook his head wildly. "I may have, sort of, left my stash with her. More like she confiscated it, but if they find it on her, needles and all, she'll get in trouble."

"Wait a minute," I said. "What do you mean, needles —are you injecting? You mean with a syringe?"

"Well, yeah." He looked like I had asked him if he liked to breathe.

My mind was spinning. He wasn't just licking the stuff? When did people start injecting it? That sounded all kinds of wrong, and probably a mile more dangerous than licking a strip of blood. I could maybe understand the attraction to the drugs in and of itself but this was another level of idiocy. What happened when people started sharing syringes? The blood would be tainted by the first user. I ground my teeth, unable to contain myself.

"Why would you inject it?" It came off more harshly than I intended.

Duncan shrugged. "It makes MagX last longer. The entire experience is, well, it's magical, for lack of a better word."

"You mean it's more magical than just licking it?" Charlie asked with much more excitement in her voice than I was comfortable with.

I glared at her and her eyes shot to the floor.

"Sorry," she muttered.

"It's freaking amazing, Char. You have no idea what you're missing out on." Duncan hopped from one foot to the other.

"Heck, you guys. You really need to get your heads on straight. It could very well kill you. I hope you looking for her isn't simply because you want your stash back, because I'll confiscate that crap myself."

Duncan's shoulders slumped. "Of course not. She's my friend, Ru."

The silence was deafening, and luckily broken as Jen strutted into the room.

"We got a girl to find, right?" Her voice was bubbly, contrasting with the energy in the room and somehow lightening my mood.

"We do," I said.

I decided to leave the discussion of injecting MagX for another time. While I didn't like it one bit, Charlie should be scared enough to at least stay clear of the drugs for a while. All I could do was focus my energy on finding Liv so that the knot still growing in my stomach could unwind a little.

We passed a few students on the steps, and Jen waved at the janitor, who was standing on a stepladder trying to fix a broken lamp.

"Maybe we can ask him?" Charlie whispered. "He's not security, so he wouldn't have the authority to turn anyone in for possession or anything. But he has to know the campus pretty well, right?"

Duncan frowned. "All right, we can ask him, but keep the details out of it."

"Hey," Jen called, already halfway to where the janitor was balancing on the stepladder.

"Good afternoon," the janitor replied. He didn't look that much older than us, perhaps in his early twenties. His chestnut-coloured hair was tied with a leather band into a low ponytail and some stubble covered his jawline.

"I guess you see a lot working here," Jen said, now standing right beside the stepladder, batting her eyes.

"Guess I do." The janitor quirked his lips up to one side. It was one of those smiles you see on toothpaste advertising; Jen was already in flirt mode, and who could blame her? Still, he was no Brendan.

"Have you seen a girl on her own today or last night maybe? Light brown hair, about this tall." Jen held her hand in the air, measuring Liv's approximate height. "Her name is Olivia, goes by Liv. Big boobs."

I almost laughed at the expression on the janitor's face. His eyes widened and he looked utterly confused. How did anyone respond to that?

"Uhm. I don't know. Have you tried her flat, assuming she lives on campus?"

"That's cool. We just thought we should ask someone who looks like he might know his way around here. We're all pretty new on campus. Know any good hideouts?"

The janitor stepped down, leaning on the ladder. "I might know a couple." He winked at Jen. "Perhaps I'll show you another time, but I don't think your girl is hiding in any of those places."

"Thanks." Jen managed to look almost coy as she folded her hands and tilted her head slightly.

"Sorry I couldn't be of more help, maybe I could get your phone number?" He cupped his hand around his chin. "In case I see her or think of something useful."

Jen tilted her head at him. "Got your phone?"

With the speed of a gunslinger from an old western film, he retrieved his phone from one of the many pockets in his trousers, a wide grin on his face.

Jen gave him her phone number while Duncan tapped his foot, clearly annoyed to have to wait for Jen to stop flirting while I, on the other hand, chastised myself for not having thought to ask Brendan for his phone number. I didn't have any way to reach him. Not that I would have called him but maybe he would have reached out to me if he had my number. It was amusing enough to watch Jen in action that I didn't mind much, but I felt for Dunc as well. His friend, or whatever she was, was still missing.

"Took you long enough," Dunc said sourly as we started towards the lake.

"A girl has needs," Jen retorted.

We continued across the grass and into the lilac archway before ending up back at Raven Court. It looked different during the day, though it still seemed like the campus equivalent to Beverly Hills. I had no idea where to start looking for Liv and my body was aching with concern. Maybe we should have alerted campus security after all? Besides, I wasn't thrilled about the fact that the only reason not to alert anyone was to cover Duncan's ass. I could understand why he didn't want us to tell, even if I didn't condone it, but if Liv was in trouble, we would have to involve authorities at some point. Not that I had any idea what kind of trouble she might have got herself into. All I had to go on was an upset stomach, which very well might be the jello shot from last night.

Jen took my arm. "We'll sniff around outside. You guys can find Diane or whoever else is home and see if anyone knows anything."

We split up. Jen wasn't kidding about the sniffing around part. She was literally sniffing her nose at anything that could be considered a clue.

"What do you expect to find from the rubbish people have left behind?" I asked.

"You never know, Red. People leave prints in different ways."

I shrugged and we continued around the large building, looking behind every piece of shrubbery we could find.

Jen was on her knees by a thick bed of thorny roses. "Ru," she called. "Look here." She parted the bush with her hands and nodded at something stuck in the slits of a drain by the wall, well hidden behind the roses.

My eyes settled on a needle, glinting as the afternoon light pierced through the gap Jen had created. A syringe.

Jen leaned in closer, wrinkling her nose. "Appears someone wanted to get rid of this."

I crouched, staring at the syringe. Was this part of Duncan's stash?

"How did you find this?" I lifted away a hanging collection of roses, and the thorns pinched my skin, a couple drawing blood. "Ouch. Why didn't you warn me about the thorns?"

Jen shrugged, still holding parts of the rose bush to the side with one hand. "I didn't even notice."

"You think this is for MagX?"

I sucked on the tiny punctures on my hand. Not that I had much experience with syringes or injections of any kind, but it didn't take a lot of MagX to reach the desired effect and the needle was small. Jen rummaged through her bag and retrieved a handful of wet wipes. An odd thing to carry around, I thought, but who was I to judge? She wrapped the wipes around the syringe and carefully placed it into her bag.

What on earth was she doing? "Shouldn't we call the police?"

"For a syringe? They would laugh at us. Still, you never know, it might be a clue." Her eyes twinkled. "So, I'm keeping it."

"Just, please don't touch it. We don't know what was in it."

"Of course not, Red."

We kept searching the area a while longer before we met up with the others again. None of us had any luck.

Liv truly had vanished.

11

DIANE AND RAHUL, THE BOY WITH THE JELLO SHOTS FROM the other night, carried a large cardboard box full of badges towards the stand, dumping it behind the table. The gig I had got to help recruit new members wasn't exactly difficult, though I had problems answering many of the questions from curious students. Heck, I was one of them. I knew as much as they did. I had, however, studied the brochures Diane had given me on the first day, and I remembered them almost verbatim. If anyone asked me something not in the brochures, however, I was clueless.

Diane patted her brow with a small towel. "Who knew badges could be this heavy, huh?" she asked, showing off a perfect row of pearly whites.

I gave her a forced smile in return. There really should be a law against people being so drop-dead gorgeous. Perfect straight and shiny hair, not a strand out of place, perfect teeth, and a swimsuit cover body. I wasn't that bad to look at myself, but my fair skin was intolerant to sunlight and I had annoying freckles on my nose. With my five foot three frame I found myself looking up at girls more often than not. Diane, however, with legs that went on forever, was simply flawless.

Rahul angled his head at me, his black hair gelled up to the extent where it looked plastered to his head. "Get any new sign-ups while we were gone?"

"Two," I replied.

"That's more than the whole of yesterday. You've made us obsolete." He grinned. "Maybe we should leave you to it."

If Diane was offended, she certainly didn't show it.

"Well done." She slapped a sticker on my denim jacket. "We're going to need people for the Whispering Willow. Strictly pro bono but we do get extra credits and direct access to archives and such. Very handy when you're working on uni assignments. Can I count on you, Ruby?"

The way she said my name made me flinch. It was sweet, like cotton candy with sugar on top, but I could swear it held a certain amount of sarcasm.

I had a moment of feeling overwhelmed. Brendan had mentioned a possible job and I was still adjusting to this new life, not to mention the new power growing inside me. Did I have time to take an unpaid job? I probably should say yes. Extra credits would look great on my job applications, and there was the added benefit of being able to dig into the MagX world more closely without arousing any suspicion.

"Sure," I said. "I don't know how much time I'll have on my hands but I'm already working on a story."

"You are?" Rahul raised his eyebrows at me, clearly intrigued.

"Yep."

I wasn't sure how much I should tell them. Charlie didn't want to pursue the matter when I had asked her, and I didn't have a lot to go on, so I decided I might as well ask the posh ones.

"I noticed someone dealing MagX at your party last night, and figured it would make a good story. Not sure about my angle yet, though. You guys know anything about that?"

Diane shifted her eyes around. The hall was brimming with students, but none were currently eyeing our stand.

"You should stay clear of that. The university won't be happy if you expose such business on campus grounds. Maybe start small, huh? Like, I don't know, do an interview with one of the lecturers or something? They always love showing off."

I frowned. "Shouldn't we always chase a lead, though? If we want to become journalists and all?"

Rahul leaned between us and dropped a handful of badges into a small box on the table. "Let people have their fun," he said. "Don't start your uni life by ruining a good thing. Lots of students use MagX to enhance their performance. There's a lot of pressure to do well, you know."

"I thought all students were tested before exams?" I said.

"In theory, yes." Rahul let out a little laugh. "But it's not like all universities have the resources of the Tour de

France. In fact, a pint of clear urine is considered a valuable commodity come exam time."

"That's gross, Rahul," Diane said and slapped him jokingly on his forearm.

These two could have been yanked straight out of a modern Downton Abbey production.

"But, I—" My voice trailed off. I wasn't going to get anything else out of these two. "Okay. I'll drop it."

They both flashed a smile at me before Diane turned her attention to the students nearby.

"Anyone want to become a journalist?" she called out. "Come on over! Best society on all campus!"

A couple of girls walked over, and Diane instantly began recruiting while I stepped back. I needed to find out where everyone got the MagX from. I wasn't so delusional that I thought I could stop the entire industry on my own. But if I found the dealers, I could possibly trace the distributors and perhaps even the very source of where it was made. With a little help, they would be exposed and the authorities could shut them down. It was a long shot, but I had to at least try. I wasn't thrilled to hear Logan's words in my head again, but he had a point. *Every big story starts with pulling that first tiny piece of string.*

"Hey," a familiar accented voice murmured.

I stepped forward as the very thought of Brendan made me immediately cheer up.

I was about to reply when Diane cut in front of me with her long, perfect legs.

"Oh, hello, B." Diane giggled as Brendan picked up a badge, shifting it between his fingers.

"This is where it all happens then?" Brendan asked.

"You know it is."

I wanted to say something but the two of them were fully engaged in some kind of friendly banter. Next to Diane, I fell easily into the background. Why was he looking at her like that? Had he even seen me standing here? Diane was a goddess, I'd give her that much, but her personality was bland. She was too chipper. The fire started growing in my veins again, eager to push out. And I wanted to let it. For a moment, I envisioned setting that golden hair of hers on fire. I breathed deeply to quiet the flames. I couldn't very well expose myself in a room full of people—or set anyone's hair on fire.

Diane took a sip of water, and without a second thought, I grabbed a handful of badges and bumped into her as I placed them in the small box. The water spilt down Diane's sheer white blouse, compelling me to give an involuntary snicker. I quickly wiped the grin off my face and turned to her.

"Oh gosh, I'm such a klutz. Are you ok?"

"I have to go change," Diane muttered, covering her chest with her arms. She turned and stalked out of the hall. She didn't even spare me a glance.

"I'm sorry," I called after her.

"Hey, Ru." Brendan finally acknowledged my presence. "Why did you do that?"

"It was an accident."

Brendan raised an eyebrow at me. He didn't appear convinced. "If you say so."

My cheeks burned. Why did I do that? I lost control of myself. Diane hadn't deserved anything like what I just did to her, for no apparent reason at all. I looked at

Brendan, who stared back. I had no idea what to say to him.

"What's up, guys?" Jen's high-pitched voice was a relief.

Rahul shot up when he saw her. "Di spilt water all over herself," he said. "She was wearing a white shirt. It was Ruby's fault."

Jen put her hands on her hips. "I see."

"It was an accident," I repeated.

"Of course it was, love," Jen said.

Rahul leaned forward, his hips pressing against the table. "You look good, Jen. Have fun last night?"

Jen shrugged and turned to Brendan. "Have you seen Olivia today?"

He squinted at her. "Olivia who? Oh, right, Duncan's friend? No, I don't think I have, why?"

"She's been missing since Diane's party. I've spent all morning talking to her flatmates, but she's not been back to her room at all."

"Perhaps she went home?" Brendan asked.

"Nuh-uh. She hadn't packed anything. All of her stuff is still in her room, including her passport. It's not like she would go back to Bulgaria without her passport."

"I'm sure there's a perfectly reasonable explanation, but I'll ask around if it helps," Brendan said.

"Thank you. We're running out of places to look. Duncan is out of his mind with worry."

Brendan nodded.

My stomach twisted into knots again. This was getting too weird. Olivia wouldn't just have vanished off the face of the earth. Not unless someone made her disappear. And if that was the case, she might be in trouble. Brendan could of course be right about the reasonable explanation, but every bone in my body told me that something was wrong and that we needed to find her soon.

"So, Ru. Charlie and I wanted to know if you have dinner plans," Jen said. "We're ordering pizza and were thinking of doing a Netflix marathon. I think we all could use some fun to take our minds off everything."

"Count me in," I said, catching a glance from Brendan. It made my skin tingle.

He waved at us. "I've got to get going. I'll let you know if I hear anything. See you around, Ruby Ruby Morgan."

He walked off and I couldn't tell if he was angry at me or maybe he didn't care enough to feel anything. Shoot. I still hadn't thought to ask him for his number. Not that he was likely to want to share it with me anyway, not after the stunt I just pulled. Maybe that job at the cinema had disappeared too. My eyes lingered on his back until he disappeared into the crowd. I had thought there was a connection between us but with what I had done to Diane, I had probably ruined whatever spark we had. No one wanted to date a bully.

Rahul found his voice again and was half sitting on the table at this point.

"Girls' night out, huh? Do you braid each other's hair, have pillow fights and stuff? I always wondered what you girls do when you're alone."

Jen rolled her eyes at me then leaned forwards, placing her palms on the table next to Rahul.

"Yes," she whispered into his ear. "All of that, and sometimes more."

"Really?" Rahul turned his face to hers.

"No, you dumbass." Jen pushed him off the table, then straightened and retrieved her phone before snapping a picture of the poor boy. *"Hashtag Notyourbusiness."* She smirked at me. "I think I'll go check on Diane. See you tonight, Ru. And if I were you, I'd find someplace better to spend the rest of my day." She strutted off in the same manner in which she had arrived.

I giggled but offered Rahul a hand, pulling him to his feet.

He was cursing under his breath, and I figured Jen was right to shove him. I also figured she was right to say I should find something better to do with my time, so I grabbed my bag.

"You can manage on your own for the rest of the fair today, right?"

Rahul glared at me. His pride was definitely hurt. "Just go already."

I didn't need him to ask me twice, and I knew exactly where I was going. To Raven Court. I had to apologise to Diane.

12

RAVEN COURT WAS AS IMMACULATE AS THE FIRST TIME I'D seen it and the smell of soap and roses radiated from the clean surfaces all over the room. How they had managed to get it so clean and tidy after the party and still be at the stand was beyond me. Unless they had hired a cleaner, of course, which was probably the case.

Diane and Jen sat on the sofa where I had sat with Brendan a few nights before. They were looking at Diane's phone, both giggling.

"He totally deserved that," Diane laughed.

"For sure. And I've got a ton of hearts already," Jen replied.

I cleared my throat and they both looked up at me. "Hi," I said, my voice breaking slightly.

"Ruby."

Diane gestured for me to sit on the sofa next to her. She had changed into a lovely maroon shirt. The fabric was smooth and it looked very fashionable. I could never afford anything like it, but Diane wore it as though it had been made especially for her. For all I knew, she probably had ten more just like it hanging in her wardrobe.

I hesitated, not quite sure where to start, then took a deep breath. "I'm so sorry about drowning you."

She raised a perfectly plucked eyebrow at me. "Not to worry, honey. I was embarrassed for a moment, but I know you didn't bump into me on purpose. I mean, I'm the one who drenched myself, not you. So, let it go already and look at the photo of Rahul."

She beamed at me, so I shook off the guilt and turned my attention to the picture of Rahul. Jen had thousands of Instagram followers, and there was already more than three hundred likes as well as a bunch of comments. The expression on Rahul's face was, admittedly, hilarious. I felt bad for him, though at the same time he kind of had it coming.

Jen pressed the button on the side of her phone and the screen went black.

"I think I'll do another sweep to see if I can find Olivia."

Diane took her hands. "Don't you think it's time you reported it? She's been missing for three days now."

I had to agree with Miss Perfection. We hadn't had any luck finding Olivia but perhaps security would. They knew this place better than any of us.

"I think she's right," I said.

"I know." Jen sighed. "Well, Dunc will just have to deal with it." She stood and held her hand out to me. I took it, determined to do the right thing at last.

"Smart choice," Diane said and blew Jen a kiss. "See you tomorrow?"

"I'll be back."

Arms linked, we hurried out the door to find our way to campus security. Of all people, Brendan stood outside the entrance to the security office with his hands in his pockets, swaying on the balls of his feet.

"B," I called as we approached him.

He smiled warily at us. "Ladies. Nice to see you again so soon."

"What are you doing here?" Jen asked.

Brendan folded a hand behind his neck. "I know the guards. They let me hang around from time to time to show me the ropes."

"Why?" I asked, finding myself curious. This was a side of Brendan I hadn't seen yet.

"Because I want to become a police officer, or maybe a detective. I don't know exactly, but I know I want to do some kind of investigative work. Protecting people. This seemed like a good start."

"But why are you lurking outside, then?" Jen frowned.

"I was contemplating whether or not I should tell them about Olivia. It's not really my business, though. Still, it doesn't sit right with me that none of you have reported it yet."

Shame welled up inside me. He was right of course, and we should have said something sooner.

"That's why we're here now."

He gave me a half-smile. "Good. I'll come with you."

The three of us stepped inside. It was a small office with a few chairs on each side of the room and a thick glass wall separating the room in half. An open counter sat in the middle of the wall and a security guard sat on the other side.

"Hey, Marty," Brendan said.

"Mr O'Callaghan," the guard replied as he closed the cover on the phone he was looking at and placed it on the counter beside him. "Want to patrol with me this evening?"

"Not tonight, I've got practice, but thank you anyway. I swung by with these two ladies. They have something to report."

Marty wrapped up a sandwich next to his phone and leaned closer to the opening. "What can I do for you then?"

I exhaled sharply and moved closer. "We want to report a missing person. Olivia Barton. No one has seen her since the day before yesterday and we're worried about her."

Marty's bushy eyebrows met in a frown before he turned to his computer and typed in a password. He clicked onward to some kind of form, glancing back at us.

"I'll need the full details. Make sure you tell me everything, even things that might seem as though they're not of importance. Understood?"

We nodded and I told Marty as much as I could, excluding the parts about MagX and what had happened to Charlie.

"So, you walked past a girl drunk out of her mind, and you didn't think to stop and make sure she got home all right?" He eyed me with what could only be judgement coating his eyes.

His words hit me like a cricket bat to the chest. His

accusation was well placed, but I couldn't tell him why I hadn't stopped. I glanced at Brendan. If what I had done to Diane wasn't enough to push him away, this would probably do the trick. I sighed and tried desperately not to sound like a cold-hearted bitch.

"I know, and I would have, but I was looking for a friend. And truth be told, I had a few drinks in me as well. Besides, I thought she was with Duncan."

I pressed my lips together. Mentioning Duncan's name was probably not the wisest decision I had made so far, and it wasn't my first screw-up of the day either.

"Duncan who?" Marty started typing Dunc's name into the form.

"Duncan Cole," Brendan said coolly.

"Ah, yes, I know Dunc," said Marty, shaking his head. "And are you sure Dunc didn't do something to her?"

What was he asking? Duncan was a mess, but he didn't strike me as someone who would hurt even a fly.

"He's her friend and he's also the one who first told us he couldn't find her," I said.

"And when was that?" Marty asked as he typed: "Known MagX user; heavy addiction; poor academic results; parents with a heavy bankroll; no siblings; a loner."

I gasped.

He was profiling Duncan. And it wasn't in Duncan's favour.

"He told us two days ago, the day after the party. He was truly concerned about her," Jen said.

Brendan scratched his head, his hazel-coloured locks weaving through his fingers.

"It could be a way of trying to look innocent. If he did do something to Liv, then—" He paused and gave me and Jen an apologetic look. "Then he knew that people would find out eventually. Maybe he thought that playing the worried friend would make him seem less suspicious."

Jen crossed her arms, and I could almost feel the resentment building up in her. I was horrified that both Marty and Brendan appeared so eager to hang Duncan for a possible crime without knowing all the facts. At the same time, I could kind of understand where they were coming from. Duncan wasn't the reliable type, and he clearly had issues on top of his heavy MagX addiction. What if he was high on MagX and had hurt Liv somehow? It could have been a drug-induced accident, and now he was trying to cover it all up. It made more sense than I wanted to admit but Jen wasn't having it.

"He wouldn't touch a hair on her head," she said. "The poor bloke is in the gutter, but he's too gentle to cause any harm. I'm telling you, you're wrong."

Marty stood and opened a door in the wall I hadn't noticed before, then stepped out to join us.

"Either way, we have to at least look at the possibility." He turned to Brendan. "I assume all the usual places have been checked?"

Brendan shrugged. "She's not been in her room, nothing was taken from the flat, she's not packed or anything. Jen, Ruby and Charlie have asked around and searched for her all over campus. She's not likely to still be sleeping off her hangover under some bridge somewhere more than two days after the party. From where I'm standing, this could be serious."

"Then this is a police matter," Marty announced. "Don't you worry. I'll notify the police, and we'll do everything in our power to find this girl. In the meantime, I advise you ladies to keep your heads down. The police will not be happy that you decided to wait this long to report this, and they certainly don't appreciate anyone tampering with evidence or butting in on an active investigation."

I nodded and nudged Jen in the side when she didn't respond.

She pinched the bridge of her nose. "Fine. We'll butt out. Just find her. Please."

Marty tilted his head at us, then glanced at Brendan. "Make sure they get home all right, yes?"

"Will do," Brendan said.

Marty was already on the phone, taking long strides as he walked under the lilac archway leading to Raven Court.

The rest of us headed the other way back to Craydon. Jen strode a couple of paces in front of us, either to give us privacy or more likely because she was pissed off about the Duncan accusations.

"People get jittery where MagX is concerned," Brendan started. "With Duncan involved, that's the first thing that comes to mind."

"But she wasn't a user. She was simply drunk," I retorted.

"Perhaps it would be best if the government knew who is a Magical and who isn't. It might be easier to keep everyone in line."

My chest tightened. Where had that come from?

"You truly believe that? People would cage—" I

almost said 'us', "them, and any Harvester would know exactly who to target. There's a reason no one displays their magical abilities."

"I suppose," he said. "Maybe. But the use and distribution of magical blood is a punishable offence. If the government had tracking on every Magical alive, then they could also protect them."

"Tracking? Like animals. Surely they won't do that." Disbelief shot through me.

"They're talking about it. I heard something about it on the news the other day. You know that priest guy, Colburn?"

"How could I not?" I said. "His face is all over the place in those ads. Congregation of Purity or whatever they call themselves."

He *was* everywhere; TV ads, whole pages in newspapers and I had even seen him on a large billboard in Piccadilly Circus. Why a religious sect would spend so much on advertising was beyond me. But I had to admit, it probably had some effect. After all, I knew very well who Jarl Colburn was, and that he viewed Magicals as a threat to humanity—the message could not be misunderstood.

"Church of Purity," Brendan said. "But yes, he was in the studio talking about how there should be new rules, if he had any say in it. I heard the Secretary of State for Justice held a hearing today about implementing new rules to make sure no Magical falls under the radar, though no one knows exactly how they are supposed to enforce it yet. I don't think they can, but we'll see."

My head throbbed. Harvesters were already breaking the law. They wouldn't care about the government promising to keep Magicals safe, and there was no way a tracking device of any sort would prevent the MagX industry from growing. It was more likely that whoever was responsible for manufacturing the drugs would get their hands on any records of Magicals, providing them with easy access to supply.

"By the way," Brendan said, making a welcome change of topic, "Nick got you an interview at the cinema next week. You more or less already got the job. They simply need to put a face to the name."

He was so close his jacket brushed against mine, and the smell of his aftershave tickled my nose. It wasn't too strong, but just the right amount, and it smelled so good I almost put my head on his shoulder to inhale the scent.

"Thank you, B. That means the world to me."

"No worries. Glad to help out." He fished his phone out. "Time you gave me your number, I should think. I'll take you to the interview, so you don't get lost on the way and miss it."

I nearly jumped on him, again restraining myself, and instead, we exchanged numbers. At least he didn't hate me. Maybe it had all been in my head? I still wasn't sure about how he actually felt about Magicals, but we could cross that bridge if we ever got there. He had said he thought the government could protect us, and even though he was wrong, it might mean that he was inclined to accept Magicals—to accept me. Mum had told me often how my dad had to work to come to terms with her abilities, and how he eventually accepted her for who she was. I didn't know if I could ever tell anyone about what I was, least of all Brendan. However,

Charlie appeared to be cool with my condition. Was it that far-fetched to think that I could share my secret with someone else? With him? After all, I was human as well as Magical.

We stopped outside Craydon Court while Jen bounced up the stairs. The silence between us was similar to that first time we had walked together like this. It was comforting in a way I had never experienced with anyone before. His gaze fixed on mine and my toes curled in my shoes.

"So," he muttered. "Fancy grabbing dinner with me tomorrow?"

"What? Like a date?" I blurted.

"Like a date."

My chest swelled as I held back my shouts of joy. "Sure." I cleared my throat and tried my best to act casual.

"Meet you by the gates at six, then? I'll take you someplace off campus."

I nodded.

"Until then, Ruby Ruby."

"Until then."

He leaned in and my lips pursed, then his arms folded around me in a hug before he let go and wandered back towards the lake. I stood frozen to the spot as my body enjoyed the internal somersaults, the scent of him still lingering in the air.

"Babe." Charlie stuck her head out of the window. "The pizza is getting cold, and I want to watch *Tales of the City*."

I unglued myself from the spot, waving at her. "Coming."

Sprinting up the stairs, I came to a halt as I reached the top. I turned, squinting my eyes at the growing darkness. Something—or *someone*—moved behind the willow by the lake. It looked like the shadow of a man. Was it —*he*—watching me? Shivers ran over my skin, and the fire in my veins burned hot. A feeling of eerie familiarity struck me once more before the shadow dissipated into thin air, as though it had never been there to begin with. The fire inside stilled yet again and I shook the shivers off.

Whatever—or whoever—that was, I had a feeling I would see it again.

13

My phone rang somewhere in the distance. Forcing one eye half-open, I peeked at the picture of Mum on the screen. I grunted and placed the phone back on the nightstand until it stopped ringing. A few seconds later, it rang again. I rubbed my eyes and reluctantly picked up the phone, snuggling under the duvet.

"Hi, Mum."

"Ruby." I could hear the smile in her voice. "I'm just being an annoying mum and checking in on you. Feels like we haven't spoken in ages. How is everything? Are you settling in all right?"

Where to start?

I wanted to tell her about Olivia, about the new power I was struggling with, and the shadow I kept seeing. But I couldn't. She would worry too much, and my London life would be cut short.

"Great," I replied. "My flatmates are really cool. Charlie is an all-round history buff, and Jen studies cultural history and feminism. Then there's Duncan. He mostly keeps to himself, though he's very nice. There are two other rooms in our flat, but no one has moved into them yet."

I hesitated.

"There's also an Irish boy I met. Brendan."

I could sense the tone of my voice changing as I said his name. I was swooning bad. It wasn't until just then I realised how much I had wanted to talk to Mum and all the things I wanted to share with her. It had been too long, and so much had happened already.

"Brendan, huh? What's he like?"

I turned it over in my head. What was he like? How could I even begin to describe him?

"He has really pretty eyes. He likes football and fencing, and he's very protective. Funny, too."

My mum went silent for a moment as if she was thinking about what I had just said. Her breathing was heavy on the other end. "He sounds like a good guy," she finally said.

"He is."

"Promise me you'll be careful, though? You can't trust anyone."

"You trusted Dad, didn't you?"

Mum chortled. "Not at first, no. And with good reason. But he came around, and when he did, I trusted him with my life, and he trusted me the same. You can never be too careful, however. Just make sure you're certain about the people you decide to put your trust in."

"I promise." I sighed, desperately wanting to change the subject. "So, how are things at the clinic?"

Mum definitely knew I was making a u-turn with

that question. Sweet as always, she let me off the hook. "The usual. A few broken bones and bruises but no major injuries in the last few days."

I had been to Mum's clinic a couple of times. For the most part, however, she had kept me far away from anything resembling a doctor's office. I never got sick, thanks to my Fae heritage. And the few times I had injured myself to the extent that any normal person would need medical attention, Mum had healed me. She never healed cuts and bruises, however, figuring I needed to experience physical pain to learn to stay clear of heights and dangerous situations. Besides, I had to maintain some kind of normalcy.

I was thankful for that.

"I hope you're not working too hard," I said.

"I've done a couple of double shifts," she admitted. "But the house is so quiet without you, plus I like my job." She paused again and gave an audible sigh. "Ruby. Don't forget that it's a long way from Cheshire to London. I won't be able to heal you if something happens, so please stay out of trouble."

"I know, Mrs Overprotective."

"I know you know, but a mother has to be clear about these things."

"You're not completely alone in the house, though. How's Kit?"

"That little rascal keeps my feet warm at night. He's clawed through the fabric of our sofa and he loves catching mice, but he is the best at cuddles."

Despite Kit clawing his way through our house, I was grateful that my mum had company. It had been a stroke of good fortune that I found him when I did. No one had claimed him either, so I figured he was part of our family by now.

"Glad to hear it," I said. "Listen, Mum, I got to go now but I'll ring you in a few days."

"Going to see Brendan, are we?" Her chuckle made me hold the phone away from my ear.

"As a matter of fact, he's taking me out for dinner tonight."

"You'll tell me all about it when we speak again?"

"Cross my heart."

"Good. Have fun on your date, darling. I'll let you go now."

We said our goodbyes and a smile spread out on my face as a text message popped up on the screen of my phone.

Still on for tonight?

My fingers ran across the screen, typing my response.

All set, O'Callaghan O'Callaghan.

Seconds later I got another reply.

Your knight awaits with your chariot, milady.

I giggled, falling back on my pillow with the phone clutched to my chest. As the euphoria subsided, I got to my feet and dug out my trainers from the heap of shoes and clothes stashed in my wardrobe. Maybe it was time to tidy everything up? I shoved the clothes as far into the wardrobe as I could and shut the door, deciding it could wait. Freshers' Fair was over, and I was glad I didn't have to spend another day with Diane and Rahul at the stands. Granted, Diane was nice and all, and I looked forward to working with her at the Whispering Willow, but something still bothered me about her. Rahul was a bit of a sleazeball, and though I kind of enjoyed his quips, it was far from enough to want to hang out with him for a whole day.

I slipped into my running outfit, put my hair up, and placed my earbuds in my ears and my phone into the phone pocket on my running shorts.

The air was crisp and the leaves were a mix of bright oranges and reds as I ran alongside the lake, Pink singing in my ears. It didn't take long before my pulse increased and I basked in the feeling of my heart pumping faster. It wasn't too early in the day but not a lot of people were up and about yet. They were probably all sleeping off a hangover from the supposed theme party at the Old Willow the night before—one the girls and I had easily skipped to binge-watch *Tales of the City* and stuff our faces with pizza and crisps.

I didn't have a lot of close friends back in Cheshire, if you didn't count Mrs Wellington, having pretty much scared off anyone I had ever been friends with. Even though I never revealed my powers to them, at least not so much that there wouldn't be any doubt, they could always tell I was different somehow. And that had scared them. The friendships I was building with Charlie and Jen, however, felt real. Charlie already knew about what I was, and she didn't care. Perhaps Jen would be okay with it too?

I skidded to a halt and pulled my earbuds out as an invisible force enveloped me, pulling my gaze to the other side of the lake. There it was again. Dark shimmers of what looked like silver tendrils and black smoke split the air, and a figure emerged. This time, the shape was undeniably a man, though his face was hidden in shadows. I had seen this before. Why couldn't I remember it, though?

I staggered back as a memory resurfaced in my mind. I couldn't have been more than three, and I had wandered off to the pond behind our house. The sense of water filling my lungs and the icy shivers of cold that pulled me under came back to me as if I was reliving the moment when I almost drowned. A drift of darkness clouded the water above me, and someone pulled me back out. The tendrils of black and silver snaked out around my body, held me as the water escaped my lungs. My head rested in the shadows.

That had been real?

As I stared at the mirage by the riverbed, it became clear that the memory was in fact very real. Whatever that thing—*he*—was, he had once saved my life. And as I thought back, more memories flooded to the forefront of my mind. The shadow had visited me more than once, watching over me, guiding me. I had thought he was an imaginary friend and at some point I had pushed him out of my mind entirely. Yet here he was. But why? What —or who—was he?

The shadows surrounding him slinked out over the surface of the lake, stretching long until they reached the other side where I stood. One single tendril rose up in front of me and I took a step back. The shadow-like form froze in the air, waiting for my move. Should I run? Why, though? I should be scared, yet whatever this was it had once saved my life. It wouldn't hurt me, I was pretty sure of that. I moved closer and the tendril brushed my hair aside, then folded around my cheek.

Loud voices pierced through my trance and the

shadows recoiled, racing back from where they had come. The figure turned its back on me. The air before him rippled and he took a step forward as the shimmers of silver and black wrapped around him, then dissipated into the ripples before everything vanished as if it had never been there to begin with.

"Ru," Charlie called, jogging in my direction, with Jen casually striding next to her. "Done with your run yet?"

"Uhm," I croaked, gathering my senses. They hadn't seen what I had? "Well, not really."

"Sure you are." Jen wiggled her eyebrows. "We're doing a photoshoot, and you, my friend, will be the star of that shoot."

"What?"

"Just play along," Charlie said, grinning. "It's all good fun."

I wasn't interested in having my sweaty morning face immortalised on Jen's Insta account.

"Can I change first please?"

"Nope. That would ruin it. I need you looking exactly like this. Strong and confident, independent woman."

"With a morning face and sweat on my brow," I grumbled.

"That too."

Charlie bumped my shoulder. "If it makes you feel any better, she's going to take pictures of me and Helen smooching later."

"Don't you mean Emma?" I shot back.

"Emma, Helen, John. What does it matter really?" She laughed and took my arm. "Come on. It'll be fun."

I blew out my cheeks and rolled my eyes at Jen. "Where do you want me?"

She tapped a finger to her lips, her gaze shifting around the lake.

"There." She pointed. "Underneath the white willow."

Reluctantly, I followed them to the willow and allowed Jen to direct me into all kinds of poses. I only put my foot down when she asked that I splash water over myself.

"This isn't Sports Illustrated," I remarked, which made Jen change her mind.

"True. Not really my style. Good call, Red."

We spent nearly an hour taking pictures before returning to our flat. Only then did I tell them about my date with Brendan.

"Cool bananas," Charlie squealed. "I knew something was going on between you."

Jen crossed her arms, looking me up and down. "Well then, time to find the perfect outfit."

She went into my room and straight for my wardrobe. A pile of clothes tumbled out to land on top of her. Charlie and I burst out laughing, smothering the small inkling of shame I felt about my messy wardrobe.

Jen gracefully shook the clothes away and began rummaging through my items.

"No. No." She held a green top in the air. "Definitely not."

"I don't have a lot of fancy clothes," I muttered. "But this is Brendan. Not sure I need anything but jeans and a band shirt."

Jen plopped onto my bed, crossing her legs. "Where did he say you were going."

"He didn't."

"He must have said something?" Charlie prompted.

"Well, he did text me." I paused. It sounded silly to say it aloud. "It said *Your chariot awaits, milady.*"

"Wicked," Charlie exclaimed. "It has to be something special."

"It's just a joke between us. It doesn't mean I need to wear a princess gown."

Jen tilted her head at me. "No, but it isn't the time for jeans either. I'll get you something from my collection again." She walked out of my room, and Charlie sat where Jen had been moments earlier.

"You like him?" she asked.

"I think I do."

"Then let Jen have her way. She'll make you look irresistible. I promise."

I sat next to her.

"It's just that I haven't been on a lot of dates. Don't get me wrong, I've had a couple of boyfriends but—" I wasn't quite sure how to say the things that were gnawing at me, though Charlie's wide eyes were surprisingly reassuring, and she already knew more about me than anyone else besides my mum.

"Every time I've got close to someone, my magic gets in the way. I'm not normal, and things tend to happen around me that makes it nearly impossible to form a connection before people storm off in the opposite direction."

"What things?"

"I—my mum has this gift which allows her to see

into people's minds when she touches them. I have it too, though not as strong, and I can't control when it happens. I only get bits and pieces. I've had some issues separating what people say out loud and what's in their heads. Whenever I've got—" I blushed. "Intimate with someone, I tend to say things that should have been kept in the confines of their minds."

Charlie pushed herself further back on the bed.

"I can see how that can get creepy." She slapped herself on her head and took my hand. "Sorry. I didn't mean it like that. I just meant that no one likes their thoughts to become public knowledge. Our thoughts are supposed to be the only thing in the world that we know for sure are our own."

A spark of something lit up in my mind as Charlie's thoughts mingled with my own. A hint of sadness and a tinge of horror flowed through me as an image of Charlie manifested in my thoughts—or rather her thoughts. A man stood over her, broken glass strewn all over the floor. Her cheek burned with pain. The thought about hitting the man back, hurting him with one of the glass shards, flitted through the memory. Charlie was scared and angry all at once, but she was so small, maybe only nine or ten.

I had seen too much, and I retracted my hand, the memory disappearing as soon as the connection was broken. My lips formed a thin line as I tried to think of what to say to her. I didn't want her to know what I had seen. It might hurt her feelings to know that she had shared such a painful memory.

Charlie raised her shoulders, a tear brimming in her eye.

"It's all right. I wanted you to see that. Wasn't sure if you would, but I'm guessing by the look on your face that you did."

"Why?" I asked.

"You shared your dirty laundry with me. I figured it was only fair that I show you mine."

"Who was that man?"

Her eyes fell. "My dad."

"Oh, Char. I'm so sorry." I wrapped my arms around her, pulling her into a hug.

"It's fine. He doesn't drink as much anymore," Charlie murmured. Then, with a burst of tiny laughter into my neck, she said, "I used to say he collected empty bottles. Sounds way better than alcoholic, right?"

Footsteps moved down the hall outside before Jen strolled back into my room. She glanced at us but ignored the obvious display of sisterly bonding.

"Here," she said, dangling a matching skirt and top in her hands. "This is pretty but not too pretty. You can easily wear your denim jacket over it, though honestly, denim is so 80s. You really should think about swapping it out for something else."

"I like my jacket." I stared at the garments. The A-line skirt matched the one-sleeved black top. Tiny strands of red decorated the edges.

"Oh, I love this," I said.

"Of course. Why wouldn't you?" Jen wiggled her hips and hung the clothes over the back of the chair by my desk.

I was mesmerized by her ability to display all that self-confidence without coming off as a narcissist.

The rest of the day went by quickly, and before I

knew where the time had gone, I was on my way to the gate to meet Brendan. I wasn't sure if I was overdressed or not poshed up enough, but the way the fabric of the clothes felt against my skin, smooth and light, made my confidence rise. Jen had done my hair, but she had gone overboard with the make-up, so I had to wash it off and do it over again myself. All in all, I felt damn good. My eyes fell on Brendan standing next to the campus gatehouse.

He was wearing jeans.

14

WELL, CRAP. I WAS OVERDRESSED AFTER ALL.

Brendan's gaze moved over me. "Milady," he said and gave me a courtly bow.

I wasn't about to return the favour with a curtsy, but I appreciated the gesture. Even if there was no chariot, no shining armour or anything. But at least Brendan was there, and that was all that mattered.

"I'm sorry," he said, giving my heart a jolt. "But that may be the prettiest sight I've seen since—oh, who am I kidding? Since ever."

Those sure were the words an overdressed lady needed. My heart continued its race from the jolt, only now it was with pure joy.

"Thank you, sire," I purred and wanted to kick myself. "Very knightly of you, although I'm pretty sure you've seen fairer maidens on your quests."

"Not at all, milady," he said. "And now I fear I have painted myself into a corner."

"Oh?"

"Everyone is going to look at you, and then at me, and then at you again, thinking what a loser I am to—"

"Stop it, B," I said, punching him on the forearm. But I enjoyed every syllable of his praise and didn't really want him to stop. "Jen insisted on the outfit, and if I had trusted her with the make-up as well, I'd look an even bigger fool than I already do."

"We could spend the evening right here, arguing who's wrongly dressed, or we could go a couple of blocks down the street and have that dinner I promised you. Come to think of it, no one will view me as the loser, since no one will even notice me, so it kind of works out after all."

Right, so now he was both charming and handsome. The fire in my veins was back, but I was quite certain it had nothing to do with my new magical power. This was magic of a different kind, and I had to admit that Brendan was the instigator.

"Dinner it is," I said and linked my arm under his outstretched one. "Where are we going?"

"Nick told me about this place, not too fancy, not too shabby. Great food," he promised.

"Nick?" I felt a slight reaction in Brendan's arm.

"He's actually a nice guy, but yes, he has a bit of a problem with the witches and wizards of the world. He's also the one who got you that job interview."

I suddenly realized I heard nothing from Brendan's thoughts, even though I held his arm. It was as if I controlled it, not wanting to read him. Yet. Not that I could mind read. It was more of a memory read than anything else. Maybe I could control the fire, too?

"And you?" I said, biting my lip.

"I think I'm a nice guy," he said.

I bumped him, laughing. "Yes, that's exactly what I meant, stupid."

"First of all, I hope to prove that I am a nice guy, but if it's ok with you, I don't want to talk about Mags tonight."

An image flashed in my head. A woman sat by a table, desperation in her eyes. No, it was more like defeat, her eyes brimming with tears. She wore a red blouse, and her hair looked a proper mess. Then a word. I tried to grasp it. *Bankrupt?* The images faded as I squeezed my eyes shut. So much for control.

We passed the corner that marked the end of White Willow campus, waited for a red bus to pass and then crossed the street. Our steps had fallen into the same rhythm, and I managed to quell the urge to read more of Brendan's memories. It felt good, both to be able to sort of control it, and not wanting to read him.

"So, what does Brendan O'Callaghan do when he doesn't hang out with the guards on campus?"

"First of all, he tries to make his parents proud, to be honest. Their dream of me graduating at White Willow also happens to be mine, so that's an easy choice. Secondly, the fencing program here is by far the best in the country."

"Fencing? Like, with swords?"

Brendan stopped, and for a moment I thought I'd said something wrong. This was the second time in minutes. What was happening to me? Why was I so anxious around him?

"Here we are, my fair one," he said, gesturing towards a door.

I hadn't paid any attention to where we were going and felt a little annoyed at my behaviour. Get a grip, Ruby, I thought to myself. Also, looking at the rest of the exterior, I concluded that I wasn't all that overdressed.

"The Halfway." I read the sign above the three windows aloud. The bottom half of the windows were frosted, making it impossible to see more than the heads of the guests by the window tables. It looked more or less like Brendan had described it—not too fancy, not too shabby. The name, though, made me curious.

"I know," Brendan said, as if he was the one reading my mind. "The owners first tried to name it *The Unsatis-fied Woman*, but that wouldn't fly by the city council. So, they compromised on *The Halfway Inn*."

I stared at him in disbelief. "Seriously? That's so tacky."

His eyes gave him away. Then he laughed. "It would be, but no, that was a lame attempt at a joke. It really was a halfway house, some decades ago, I think. Shall we?"

He held the door for me, and I stepped inside. Some twenty tables filled the main area of the restaurant, and a gallery seemed to house four or five more. Under the gallery were a bar and two swing doors through which waiters constantly came and went.

"Welcome," said a smiling woman—she couldn't be more than a year or two older than me. "Party of two?"

"I have a reservation," Brendan replied. "O'Callaghan."

The girl stepped behind a small desk and looked at a computer screen. "There you are, Mr O'Callaghan. If you'd like to follow me, please."

She walked towards the stairs at the end of the bar, and we followed her up to the gallery where she showed us to our table. "Your waiter will be here in a jiffy. Care for a drink while you look at the menu?"

Brendan nodded before I had a chance to reply. "Yes, please. Make it light and sparkly, perhaps?"

The girl smiled and disappeared. Brendan held the chair for me, and I sat. It felt a bit awkward looking down at the other guests, their food in particular, so I looked out the window instead. A drizzle had started as we entered the restaurant, and with the streetlights on, it looked quite romantic. Or maybe it was just what my heart told me. After all, I was on a date. And although Brendan was probably no more than twenty, it felt like my first grown-up date.

After a few minutes, I understood why Nick—and Brendan—would like this restaurant. Granted, it didn't come off as particularly posh, but I had half expected the menu to consist of French words and prices above my budget. I had every intention of going Dutch on the bill, so I was relieved to see an array of burgers, ribs, fajitas and five different types of fried chicken.

"Students must love this place," I said, only now noticing the clientele being mostly twenty-somethings, the usual hipsters, and even a couple of girls I was sure I had seen at Diane's party.

The food was everything Nick had promised, and although I had never been a huge fan of the Big Mac, it had been my go-to choice at McDonald's. Something told me it would be a while before it tempted me again, having bit into the moist, savoury burger they named *Old Smokey*.

"I wouldn't mind coming here again," Brendan said, biting into his *Southern Belle,* with extra bacon.

"I hereby vow to never order a Big Mac again," I said. "This is pure magic."

"Fitting for the company then," Brendan said, winking at me.

I almost choked on what the menu described as applewood smoked cheddar. What did he say? Did he know?

"I don't want to sound too cheesy, Ruby, but what the hell. I really like you, and sitting here looking at you is a way better magic feeling than what any Mags or drug can provide."

So there it was. He didn't know about me, but his undertone was clear. He was too good to be true.

"We weren't going to talk about them," I said, feeling the taste of betrayal in my mouth by calling Mags *them.* "But I get the impression they're not your favourites?"

He washed his mouthful down with two large gulps of his beer, his eyes never leaving mine. "No."

Short and to the point. Ok, I'd leave it at that, then. Just enjoy the evening, and accept that Brendan and I would never be.

"I guess most of them are ok," he continued. "But in general, I think the world would be better off without them."

I said nothing, although the journalist in me screamed and shouted a million follow-up questions in my head.

"It's just that I've had a bad experience." He picked one of the fries from the little wicker bag in front of us, dipped it in the chilli ketchup, and bit off half.

It killed me to say nothing, but I was determined to leave it up to him to speak. At least about this.

He sighed. "I'm sorry to kill the mood, Ruby."

"Not at all. I want to know you," I said, hoping he didn't notice the shiver in my voice. "I really want to know you, B."

I lay my hand on the table, close enough for him to grab it if he wanted.

He did. The surge of electricity through my body made it almost impossible not to look into his mind. But only almost—I held it back, nearly cheering to myself. And then I looked into his eyes. If I had thought they were stunning before, that was nothing compared to now, with tears in them. Not really tears, but a thin veil of moisture, bringing the colour to an even darker, more intense, shade of blue.

"And I want to know you, too, Ruby," he whispered. "I really want to."

If someone had told me we'd sat like that for forty-eight minutes, I would have believed them. In reality, it was probably just five or ten seconds, but the moment changed something in me. It confirmed something. My blood was on fire, albeit not literally. Or maybe even literally.

"My sister dated a Mag," Brendan said, jolting me out of my haze. His gaze drifted towards the dark street outside. "A proper knobhead, although he probably seemed nice in the beginning. Teagan's two years older than me and was already well into her bachelor studies right here at White Willow. Oliver worked at *The Barrister*, a coffee bar on campus."

I nodded, both because I had seen the sign, thinking

it was a pun on barista and that maybe it catered to the law students, and because I didn't want to say something to break his stride.

"Somehow he managed to convince Teagan to run off with him. They just showed up at our house one evening in the middle of the spring semester. Teagan flashed a diamond ring at my ma' and told my parents about his and Teag's plans to buy a house in Spain. Oliver had been appointed the head of a hotel on the Sun Coast, and my sister would run the marketing side of things."

Brendan still held my hand, his grip tightening a bit as he spoke. I made a mental note to confirm my ability to control the mind-reading when I was back with Charlie and Jen later.

"Anyway, to make a long story short, he fooled my parents to invest all their money in the hotel. Or rather, in his bank account, since he convinced them that was the best way. There's no way my da' would agree to something like that. He has always been the calm, thinking, and re-evaluating type. Never made a decision in business unless he was sure he had double and triple checked everything. Then this loser does some Jedi mind tricks on my parents and takes off with all their money. And their daughter, who he also used his mind-controlling powers on."

"What about you?" I asked.

"I was in China, three weeks of training with the Chinese fencing team. The wanker would've turned my mind inside out as well, had I been home."

His grip was starting to hurt me, but no way was I going to stop him now.

"When I came home, it was three days after Teagan

and Oliver had run off, I think. Ma' just sat there. Da' had picked me up at the airport, and already I knew something was off. Ma' had never missed a chance to greet me with a hug until then. When I walked into the dining room, she didn't even look up."

She wore a red dress and her hair was a mess, I thought.

His voice cracked. "'*We're bankrupt,*' she whispered. '*All our money is gone, Brendan.*'"

I closed my eyes and swallowed hard. A Mind-controller. Mum had always warned me about those. Not that they could do anything to my mind—apparently they only had power over humans' brains, but they could certainly harm others, especially if they were powerful.

"So, when Teagan and Oliver left, his effect on their minds wore off?" I asked. This would at least mean he wasn't very powerful, if I had understood Mum correctly.

"Hm?" Brendan said, refocusing on me. "Yes, they came to themselves the next day, Da' told me. Why?"

"Just something Charlie said about magical powers wearing off," I said, hoping again he didn't catch the tone of my voice. "Did they contact him? Or maybe the police?"

"Nobody knows where they are. The hotel, *La Playa Soleil* or some shit like that, doesn't exist, of course. He's got my Teagan stashed somewhere, holding her under his spell. Or maybe he dumped her after he got all the mo-ney."

"Oh, Brendan. I'm sorry, but you're hurting my hand."

He let go, his eyes shocked. "Shit, Ru! I didn't know—"

"That's ok, B. I understand completely." I had to stop him before his impressively strong hand broke a bone or two in mine. "So, that's what a fencing hand feels like."

Neither of us managed to finish our meals, both because of the sheer size of them but also because of B's story. I could see why he hated Mags, although it wasn't fair to include all other Mags in Oliver's wake. Still, people tended to judge by their personal experiences, as I had myself, I was sure.

After a failed attempt to go Dutch, I accepted Brendan paying the bill on the condition that I was allowed to pay for the next date.

"So, Ruby Ruby Morgan," he said outside the restaurant, while the slight drizzle in the air dampened my hair. "That implies there is going to be a second date?"

Yes, I think I'd like that, was what I was about to say as a heavy gust of wind blew through the street. The "Today's Special" blackboard collapsed and skidded across the pavement, the rest of the words flashing in front of me just long enough for my mind to register them: "You're special to us!"

"Wow, that wasn't on the forecast." Brendan pulled me into his arms. "Better wat—"

He went limp for a second, before collapsing to the ground, much like the blackboard sign. I tried holding on to his arm, but couldn't stop him from hitting his head on the pavement.

"Brendan!" I fell to my knees, scooping my hand under his head. It was wet and warm.

Before I could call for help, someone grabbed my

arms and started pulling me away from Brendan. I tried to resist, but he was way stronger than me. Then a hand covered my mouth.

"Don't fight it, or I'll cut your throat, you monster," a man's voice whispered in my ear.

Even if I wanted to obey him, my instincts did not. In my right hand, a small globe of light and magic formed, and I threw it back at whoever idiot had chosen this night to rob a Fae.

"That won't work, Miss Morgan," the voice spat. "This will, however."

A sharp sting of pain shot into my neck, extinguishing the flames. I screamed into his hand, darting my eyes from side to side, hoping to see someone—anyone—coming to help. But the street was empty, apart from my unconscious and bleeding date.

"I'll give you one more chance, Ruby. Will you do as I say, or do you want the whole knife in your neck?"

"I—I'll do as you say," I whispered.

"Excellent. Now, we'll go slowly backwards for a few more yards, and then I will—"

"You will do absolutely nothing," said another voice, this one also a man's, but a lot deeper. "In fact, you can cease to exist."

A flash of light lit up the whole street like a burst of lightning. Then the arm around my waist was gone. I whirled around, but no one was there. Except for a knife, which came to rest on the ground as if it had just landed. The edge was smeared with blood—my blood.

"Go help your boyfriend, Princess," said the deep voice.

A towering silhouette moved towards me. My

subconscious must have thought it was a tree or some-thing in my peripheral vision. The shape was that of a man's, but at the same time, it wasn't. It wasn't a shadow like the one following you on a sunny day, but there was still no better word to describe it.

A shadow.

"He must not know of this," the voice said. No, the shadow said. The voice came from inside it. "Heal his wo-und, but don't let him know, Princess."

"Who are you?" I asked, only now noticing that the wind was gone. In fact, there had been no wind other than the gust that blew the restaurant's sign over.

The shadow stopped maybe six feet away from me. It's head, or at least where I figured the head would be, to-wered over me.

"Go, Princess. We'll meet again."

Then it—he—dissolved like bubbles of black smoke.

I stood for a moment, trying to grasp what had happened, when I heard the engine of a car up the street. The headlights hadn't reached Brendan's body yet, but it would only be seconds. I ran the few yards back to him and knelt beside his slumped body.

Heal his wound.

Even as scary as the scene was, I still enjoyed the feeling inside when I summoned my healing powers. It was always my greatest joy, ever since I was three and healed my first goldfish. The warmth inside my body when I summoned the magic was like nothing else, not even the firepower I had to learn more about. My hand touched Brendan's head again, and I let the magic flow through the warm, wet blood and into the wound.

"What happened? Is he ok?"

A young couple came out of the restaurant just as I stopped the healing.

"I—he fell. I think he tripped on that sign," I said, nodding towards the broken frame by the wall.

"Hnggg," said Brendan. "What the—"

"Shh," I said. "You hit your head. Lie still for a minute, ok?"

He looked up at me, puzzled. "Ruby?"

I smiled back at him. "Oh? Did you hit it so hard you forgot about Ruby Ruby?"

Brendan rubbed the back of his head with his hand and started to sit. "Is that blood?" Shock filled his eyes as he noticed the cut on my neck. "You're hurt! What the hell happened?"

I laughed, happy to escape having to explain why he was bleeding without any wounds. "I'm sorry, but I think I might have rubbed my blood into your hair. It must have been a splinter from the sign you tripped on or something. It's no biggie."

He tilted his head and squinted ever so slightly, as if he knew I wasn't telling the truth.

I tried not to show him that I had picked up on his scepticism. It was fair, and a natural reaction on his part, after all. I had lied. But that was what the shadow had told me to do. *He must not know*, it had said. And somewhere inside me I knew the right thing was to follow its advice.

"The answer is yes," I said.

"Huh?" Brendan scrambled to his feet.

I looked at the young couple, who still stood staring at us. The girl pulled the boy's arm, whispering that they should leave. When they were gone, I turned back to the confused Brendan standing in front of me.

"Yes, I hope there is a second date." I winked at him. "If you dare to take your chances, that is."

In my head, I was frantically trying to understand what had happened to the man who had tried to—well, what was he trying to do, exactly? Kidnap me?

15

The living room was clouded with smoke, wafting from the kitchen on the other side of the room. The smell of bacon and eggs lay heavy in the air. Charlie was frying the bacon to a crisp while wiggling her hips to 'Bohemian Rhapsody' echoing off the walls. I wasn't complaining about her making us all breakfast, though. Neither was Jen or Duncan. And Charlie sure had some moves.

"Dig in," she chirped as she placed the plates on the table.

My mouth watered as I stared at the meal: sausages, bacon, eggs, mash, tomatoes—and no beans, as per my request. I filled my fork and shoved the food into my mouth, then nearly choked on it as a loud banging issued from outside our door.

"Sod it all," I coughed.

Jen stood. "I'll get it."

She disappeared into the hallway and opened the door, its hinges creaking slightly.

A male voice followed, though I couldn't decipher the words, and then Jen popped her head round the doorway.

"You need to come here," she said.

We all left our delicious food behind and went to the front door.

I staggered as my eyes fell on the policemen in the doorway. One was almost as wide at the waist as he was tall, the other looked more like a young Jason Statham. Broad shoulders and toned muscles were visible even through his blue shirt.

"Ladies," the plump policeman offered, greeting Charlie and me. "And you are Duncan Cole, I presume?" He raised his eyes, his head turned down to a notebook in his hands.

"None other," Dunc said, fidgeting with his sleeves. The policemen put him on edge, which was understandable considering the circumstances.

"We're here about the disappearance of one Ilyana Makarova," the Statham look-alike said sternly. "I'm Police Constable Paddock. This is my colleague, PC Fernsby."

"Iliyana?" I asked.

"Olivia's real name," Dunc muttered under his breath.

"Oh," I said, puzzled.

"May we come inside?" Fernsby asked while Paddock was already two steps beyond the threshold.

We escorted them into the living room, where Charlie cleared the table with impressive speed. I could almost hear my stomach grumble at the sight of the food being carried off.

No one sat down, however. Apart from Jen, who casually pulled out a chair, straddling it the wrong way around before leaning her arms on the back.

"Which one of you is Ruby Morgan?" Fernsby asked as he brought up a pen.

I raised a hand in the air.

"We understand you were the last person to see Miss Makarova, is that correct?" Fernsby shifted his gaze to the chairs and took a seat next to Jen, placing his notebook on the table.

"As far as I know," I replied.

Paddock eyed me with what I could only describe as contempt. "And you neglected to tell anyone about it for three days?"

I sighed. The whole truth wasn't an option, but I figured I should try to stay as close to the truth as I could.

"I know. I'm sorry about that."

"Were you aware that her papers were forged? She wasn't here legally."

I shook my head in disbelief and shot Duncan a cold stare. It made a lot more sense now.

"Miss Morgan, we need you to walk us through everything you saw or heard that night," Paddock said. "And make sure you tell us everything."

My thoughts scrambled as I tried to recall the night of Olivia's—Iliyana's—disappearance, starting with our arrival at Raven Court. I walked the officers through the events, excluding bits and pieces along with my narrative.

"Charlie had a falling out with this girl and I went to check on her," I said. "That's when I saw Liv, or whatever her name is, sitting by the wall outside. She was barely awake."

"Was there MagX at the party?" Paddock asked, leaving me tongue-tied.

What was I supposed to say?

Charlie put a reassuring hand on my back, smiling broadly at the officers. "Not that any of us knows," she said, turning her Plymouth-Brazilian charm on. "That shit is illegal. I don't know anyone who would be foolish enough to bring panels or anything like that to a public place."

The girl sure knew how to lie through her teeth.

"But you do know of people using it?" Paddock shot Duncan a look.

None of us said anything to that, and I decided to try to move the conversation back to the real issue.

"Liv—sorry, Ilyana, was just drunk," I said. "I did go back to check on her, but by the time I got there she was gone."

"Anything else you would like to share about that night?" Fernsby asked, flipping over a page in his notebook.

"Actually," Jen said. She shrugged at me. "We did find something. Didn't think much of it, and I probably shouldn't have taken it, but it made me curious." She stood and walked out.

The silence was suffocating as we all waited for her to return. Fernsby had a gentle expression on his face but Paddock couldn't look more like a pillar of ice if he tried.

"Here." Jen walked back in and placed the syringe she had found on the table next to Fernsby's notebook.

Paddock stepped around the table, placing his palms next to the syringe, a deep frown shading his eyes. And then—was that a brief smile? Why?

"I should throw you in the nick for this." He wiped the smile off and gritted his teeth instead.

There was a split personality if I ever saw one. What was up with him?

"What were you thinking, bringing this home with you? Bloody hell." Paddoc's brows knitted together.

"Now, now," Fernsby said, retrieving a plastic bag from his pocket.

He placed his hand inside the bag and grabbed the syringe before he turned the bag in on itself and zipped it closed.

"Thank you," he said to Jen. "We will make sure to check this out. We don't have a lot of leads and this could certainly help, assuming it has anything at all to do with Miss Makarova."

Paddock was seething, his reaction far too strong for what had occurred. I had the sudden urge to touch him, to try to read his thoughts. I wasn't sure why but there was something about him that bothered me, besides his cold exterior. The officers were killing it with the good cop/bad cop routine.

"Now," Fernsby said as he pocketed the evidence bag with the syringe. "Mr Cole. Would you be so kind as to sit?"

Duncan was shaking, his motions jittery. It had probably been a while since his last fix. I liked Dunc, despite his addiction, and it pained me to see what magical blood had done to him. He sat, almost missing the seat of the chair, easing his way into it.

Paddock straightened, and a weird quirky motion tugged at his lips again. "How long have you known Miss Makarova?"

Duncan's eyes were fixed on his hands, knitted together on the table. "About a year, I think."

"She's been staying with you?"

"For a while, yeah."

"And what is the nature of your relationship?"

Duncan licked his lips, shifting his weight in the chair. "We're friends."

"You sure about that? No romantic relationship or unrequited feelings, perhaps? No common drug abuse or anything?"

What was Paddock getting at? This didn't bode well for Duncan at all. I felt sorry for him. At the same time, however, the questions weren't completely out of line.

"No, nothing like that," Duncan stuttered.

"You were the last person to be seen with her, aside from Miss Morgan. Why did you separate?"

Duncan pulled his sleeves over his hands. "I was going to meet someone."

"Another so-called friend?" Paddock hissed.

"You could say that. Liv didn't want to come, so I told her I'd see her after."

"And did you?"

"No, she was gone by the time I got back."

Paddock leaned forwards, bumping his fists down on the table to stare at Duncan. "Are you absolutely sure you didn't see her again that night?"

Duncan raised his gaze, steadier than he had been since the officers showed up. "Yes!"

"And if, say, you were high, would you still be certain you didn't see her?"

Duncan's gaze shifted again. "I—no, I—she's my friend. I spent all night looking for her, and I've been looking for her ever since."

"And yet, you neglected to report her missing."

The officers asked a bunch of other questions and kept coming back to Duncan, pressuring him about his MagX addiction and asking him several times if he hadn't seen Ilyana again. His answer was always the same, and yet they didn't appear to be satisfied with his response. Especially not Paddock.

After what felt like all morning had gone by, Fernsby put his notebook in his shirt pocket.

"That would be all for now, I should think. Right, PC Paddock?"

Paddock only grunted in response as Fernsby rose from the chair.

"I think you should know that another girl is missing," Fernsby said. "Her name is Corinne Jacobs, and she's listed as a possible Magical. We suspect she's some kind of Elementalist. We're not sure if her magic has anything to do with her disappearance, or if it's connected with Miss Makarova being gone, but I urge you all to be extra vigilant. Do not go anywhere alone. We have advised the headmaster of the university to impose a curfew as well, and you are all to stay inside after nine pm until this matter has been resolved."

Curfew? And a Mag was missing? My chest tightened, and I all but gasped for air. How was this connected? Maybe Fernsby was right, and there was no connection, but still, maybe there was. The way they had pressed on about MagX wasn't helping my nerves either. I couldn't very well close my eyes to the obvious. If a Magical was involved, MagX might have something to do with it. And even though Duncan was adamant about Olivia's preference for alcohol, perhaps he was lying about that too?

"We thank you for your time," Fernsby said.

Paddock stomped out into the hallway before turning back to us.

"And don't go running off," he said. "Especially not you, Mr Cole. We'll be back if and when we need to talk to you again."

The officers left and I let out a breath, clutching my chest.

Charlie was quick on her feet, however. She grabbed the plates of now-cold breakfast and put them back on the table. "Not as good anymore, but I think we could all use the energy."

We ate in silence while I turned everything over in my head. The police undoubtedly suspected Duncan, and part of me was inclined to suspect him, as well. Not that I thought he was lying, though he hadn't been entirely truthful about Olivia either, and if he had been under the influence of MagX, he might not even remember what he had done. Then again, another girl was missing, and if the two cases were linked, Duncan probably didn't have anything to do with it. Unless I was reading him all wrong and he wasn't as innocent as he seemed. A thought occurred to me and I put my fork down.

"Dunc," I said, meeting his gaze. "Do you know if Liv is a Magical?"

He played with the leftovers of his food. "Nah, she's just an illegal immigrant," he said.

I decided to drop it. For now. But I was going to get to the bottom of this, no matter what. If the other missing girl, Corinne, really was a Magical, then I had to find out why she had disappeared and who might have taken her. For all I knew, it could be the same man that had attacked me outside the restaurant yesterday. Now, that was an unsettling thought. Also, if the shadow had made that man disappear, it wouldn't make it any easier to find the missing girl. Or girls.

I returned to my room after helping Charlie with the dishes. I opened my laptop and sat down on my bed. Where to start, though? I searched for MagX, and millions of results popped up. It was mostly articles about the revelation of Magicals in the world, people who had died from an overdose, as well as a bunch of medical sites listing the pros and cons of magical blood. It was definitely the old needle in a haystack, only this haystack was enormous.

There was a knock on my door, and Charlie peeked inside. "May I come in?"

I nodded, closing my laptop, and Charlie came to sit next to me.

"What are you doing?"

"Nothing."

Charlie lowered her glasses to the tip of her nose and tittered. "The truth shall set you free, Morgan."

I gave a short laugh. "All right. If you must know, I'm trying to figure out anything I can about the missing girls and the connection to MagX."

Charlie wiggled herself close to the wall, plopping one of my pillows behind her back.

"Right. Count me in."

"Really?"

"I know I said I wasn't interested, but this has got out of hand. I didn't understand the severity before but I'm beginning to. Also, I could have easily been one of those girls. I don't believe Duncan for a second when he says Liv–slash–Ilyana wasn't a user. There is definitely a link here."

I breathed a sigh of relief and opened my laptop again.

"Thank you. I don't know where to start searching, though. There's too much to sift through, and nothing directly related to the White Willow disappearances. Doesn't seem to have reached the press yet."

"Oh, it will. But girls go missing all the time. Once they confirm a link to MagX, however, you can bet your cute arse that this will reach the headlines."

The feeling of dread settled in my stomach.

She was right, of course. Disappearing Magicals was a common thing now, and the politicians were busier arguing than actually doing anything about it. The press almost seemed to have lost interest, but two girls from the same university would surely get the journalists' attention. Not to mention Mum's. She would find out about the disappearances at some point, and that would be it for my short-lived London adventure.

Unless the culprit was caught first.

"Any ideas?" I said.

"A few." Charlie gestured at my laptop and I handed

it to her. "Right, we'll need to dig deep. First, though, any idea what an Elementalist is?"

"It's a Mag with the ability to control an element, I think. I never met one. Not a real one at least, though I've seen an Elemental power in use."

The memory of the earth moving below my feet, and Susan's body in the rubble afterwards, resurfaced. I forced it to the back of my mind in fear I would start sobbing if I thought about it for too long. "Not that I've met a lot of Magicals as far as I know, and Mum always said she thought most of the Elementalists stayed behind in Avalon, so I'm guessing it's quite rare on Earth."

"Wait. What? Avalon? You mean THE Avalon? As in Arthur and the sword in the fudging stone Avalon?"

"Well, yes, in a manner of speaking. Although that sword was never in Avalon, I think—you mean Excalibur, right? Anyway, there's more to the legend than what you find in human stories, but yes, Avalon is very real. Or was. It's sort of—lost," I said regretfully.

Charlie bounced to her knees, almost sending my laptop flying to the floor. She grabbed it before it went off the edge of my bed, but her eyes were fixed on me.

"So wait, Miss Morgan." She wiggled her eyebrows. "Anything else you'd like to share? Your name cannot be a coincidence, then, right?"

Charlie had turned into a five-year-old in a candy store, but it felt good not to hide who I was. I had to give her something, and for the first time in my life, I could talk about my heritage with someone other than Mum and Dad.

"It's not," I said, doing my best not to giggle at her wide eyes. "My mum and I are descendants of Morgana

Le Fay, the first of all Faes and ruler of Avalon. The Morgana blood runs strong in our family, or so my mum says anyway. That is, until my dad was the first human to father a child in our line."

"Mental!" Charlie exclaimed. "It's all real! You have to tell me everything!"

"I will, but perhaps not all at once, though? We have more important things to do."

"Right." The glow from the screen lit up Charlie's face as she opened the laptop again. "Watch me do my magic. It might not be Avalonian, but I bet you don't know how to get into the darkest corners of the web the way I do. First, let's close this browser and use a safe one instead."

This girl was full of surprises. Her typing was just short of super speed as she navigated us deeper into the web than I knew possible.

"Where did you learn all this?" I asked.

Charlie looked up at me while continuing to type at a blistering speed. "Here and there," she said. "There was this coding club for kids, and it was free. Piano lessons were not, so I played my own kind of keyboard. Maybe I'll tell you about it some time." She hunkered over the computer again.

"Magic market," she mumbled after a while.

"What now?"

"Here." Charlie pointed at the screen. "It's huge. See? You can buy magical trinkets, learn spells, find others with similar interests." She clicked onwards a few times. "Not to mention get in contact with MagX dealers."

"Holy Lady of the Lake!" I said.

"Don't tell me you swear in Avalonian, too?"

"That's not swearing," I said. "And I don't know the first word in Avalonian. Guess I picked up some of Mum's expressions. But never mind that, you are a freaking genius." I nodded at the screen, thoroughly impressed.

"They don't call me Einstein for nothing."

"Do they, though?"

"They should," she said, feigning insult.

Something caught my eye. It was an ad on the sidebar. *MagX is yesterday's drug*, it said. *Want to feel PURE magic?* I frowned, but Charlie had already clicked onto another page about something called Harvester Academy before I could think to ask her about the ad.

"Holy macaroni!" Charlie gaped. "It's a recruitment agency for Harvesters!"

"Can you dig into it?" I asked.

She opened a little window, typed some code into it and made a few more clicks, then shook her head. "Nah, this is heavily fortified. It's 3FA."

"Right," I said. "Hate when that happens."

She laughed. "Sorry. 3FA means three-factor authentication, which in layman's terms means I can't get in. That's right—not even I."

An academy for Harvesters? That sounded all kinds of wrong, though I supposed Harvesters didn't just appear out of thin air. I guess I always thought they were more like dealers, working on their own volition. How delusional. This was a bigger network than I had imagined. I would have to ask Mum if she knew about it, but not now. At least not until the mystery of the missing girls had been solved.

We sifted through as much of the magical market as

we could, though none of it made us any wiser on the subject of the missing girls, so we decided to leave it for now and try again later.

Jen stopped by to tell us we were going to the Old Willow. She didn't ask, merely stated it as fact. And as had become our usual routine, we did as Jen said. As I was getting ready for our night out, I got a text from Brendan asking if we were going to the Willow. I hadn't even had a spare moment to think about him all day. The tension in my chest subsided at the thought of seeing him again, however.

Our date hadn't exactly been daisies and rainbows, but it had brought me closer to him, and I was eager to see him again.

Deciding to push my troubles aside, I focused on Brendan to cheer me up, wrapping the encounter with the police and all the stuff we had found on the magical market to the back of my mind. I couldn't completely free myself from the thousand questions buzzing in my head, but I wasn't about to let it ruin my night either.

As we strolled past the lake on our way to the Old Willow, my gaze darted to the other side where the shadow had been the last time I saw it. That was an entirely different nest of worms to uncover, too.

Jen linked her arm in mine and whispered into my ear.

"Shake it off, Red. Nothing bad will happen to you while I'm around."

I leaned closer to her. "My guardian angel, are you?"

She bumped her hip into mine. "Something like that. Now—" She stopped momentarily to pinch my cheeks. "You look perfect. Let's go and leave that Brendan of yours slobbering like a wet rug on the floor. He won't be able to refuse a kiss from you looking like this."

Charlie didn't say anything, but her expression was reassuring. I wasn't quite as confident, although the girls helped. I did want tonight to be about Brendan. And whatever came next, at least I had friends by my side to back me up.

16

THE FIRST LECTURE OF MY ACADEMIC LIFE HAD JUST finished, and if I was being honest with myself, I was a bit disappointed. It was just some introductions to the various courses in the journalistic programme and the professor, Zhang, sounded quite monotonous. Still, I was sure the pace would pick up and that I'd soon be flooded with work and deadlines.

As I entered our flat, I was met with music streaming from Charlie's room. I ditched my backpack on my bed and went to say hello. She sat by her desk, her fingers tapping away at the small wireless keyboard. She had been very persistent about my old laptop being junk, and that her beloved iMac was much better suited for browsing the magic market on the dark web.

I dumped down on the bed and rested my head on the backpack, my fingers brushing over my lips, recalling the night before. Once again I had missed my chance at a kiss, but I could almost taste it. My entire body was aching to be near him again.

Even knowing how he felt about Mags, valid reasons or not, I couldn't dictate my feelings, and they were fully latched onto the dashing Brendan O'Callaghan.

"Ru!" Charlie shouted.

"Huh? Why are you screaming at me?"

"I've said your name like five times already."

"Oops." I couldn't stop myself from grinning.

"You've got the BB, haven't you?"

"The BB?" I looked at her, raising an eyebrow.

"The Brendan Bug. And you have it bad, baby."

"So bad," I admitted and forced myself to a sitting position. "Find anything?"

"Ok, fine, let's change the subject, then."

"You came to me, Charlie."

"Oh, right. Well, mostly the same we looked at yesterday. I tried all night to access the Harvester Academy server, thinking we might find some records of something useful, but no luck in that department. That site has better security than the Pentagon." She folded the screen down a little to let me have a look. "I did find a couple of interesting things, however, though I'm not sure if any of it means anything."

I squinted, not able to read it all from my bed, so I stood and stepped to Charlie's side.

The page was filled with ads and banners, surrounding what appeared to be chat forum topics. *Cheap and clean MagX, MagX Swapping, Camelot Inc., MagX Emporium* and dozens more.

It was shocking. Disgusting. And one particular ad caught my attention. "PureX," I mumbled. "What the hell is that?"

"From what I gather, sifting through the forum, it's a new drug on the market."

"A new drug?" I swallowed hard. "As in a magical drug?"

"It says here that PureX is a pure form of MagX, not as easily tainted as the latter. This one guy says the effect lasted for days."

"Holy Lady," I exclaimed, reading comments from the thread. "Manufactured from pure magical blood. No half breeds here." My breath caught in my throat. This was bad, really bad.

Charlie patted me on my arm. "It seems to be very rare, though, judging by the fact that they literally auction the blood away to the highest bidder. See?" She pointed at a section on the screen.

The last vial of PureX had been sold for millions of pounds. It definitely was a commodity. It hit me like a freight train. Pure blood could only mean it was taken from pure Magicals—like Mum!

"You all right, Ru?"

I shook my head, trying desperately to collect my thoughts. "I—I think I need to talk to my mum about this."

"If you think that will help," Charlie said reassuringly, though I wasn't so reassured. "Unfortunately, I've not seen anything yet that might link back to whatever has happened to—what was her name again?"

"Iliyana," I said. "Ilyana Makarova. But probably easier to keep calling her Liv."

"True."

A Nightwish song blasted through our flat, and Charlie and I went out into the hallway. Jen's door was open, and she was sitting on the windowsill, doing her make-up.

I walked over to her Alexa and turned the sound of Floor Jansen's booming voice down.

"Going somewhere?" I asked.

"I am indeed." Jen winked at me, her eye shadow covering half of her eyelids. "I've got a date with the janitor tonight."

Charlie leapt onto Jen's bed. "Seriously. He's super hot!"

"I know, right?"

"I wish I was going on a date, too. Between you and Ru, I'm starting to feel like an old maid." Charlie pouted, though her eyes were bright with mischief.

I shared a glance with Jen, and we both burst out laughing.

Jen was the first to collect herself. "Maybe if you start by remembering their names, you could move on to an actual date. It's not like you've been lacking attention or anything."

Charlie cradled Jen's pillow, giving Jen a wry smile. "You're right. It's just, I want that spark. That human connection. I don't much care where it comes from, but until I find it, I'll enjoy the company of whoever swings my way. Lord knows I swing every which way there is." She shrugged. "Besides, relationships are complicated."

"Yeah, you're a real modern-day hippie," I quipped, and we all started laughing again.

It was so good to feel like I had an actual connection with these girls, as if we would be friends forever.

Somewhere in me, however, I had doubts. Someday

they would both discover the extent of what I was capable of if we stayed close. And if I were them, I would think twice about staying friends with me. I sighed, shoving the devil's advocate in me to the back seat. It might not end that way. They might both accept me—all of me. I clung to that sliver of hope with every fibre of my being.

"Hey," Charlie said. "Didn't you say you had to ring your mum?"

I slapped myself on my forehead. "So I did. Excuse me."

Moving back to my room, I shut the door firmly behind me and stuffed my earbuds into my ears, climbing onto the windowsill with the phone in my lap as I hit the caller button. It rang three times before Mum picked up.

"Hello, darling." She sounded as warm as ever. "I was wondering if I would hear from you today."

"Hi, Mum. I thought I should check in on you, being the annoying overprotective daughter and all."

That prompted a chuckle from my mum. "Glad to hear it," she replied.

"How's Kit?"

"The little rascal is growing, and he loves to cuddle. But stop deflecting and tell me what I want to hear. How was your date with the dashing Brendan? Tell me everything!"

Biting my lip, I knew I had to bend the truth a little. I seemed to be doing that a lot lately.

"He took me to a place called the Halfway," I said. "Best burgers you will taste in your entire life."

"I do like burgers," Mum teased.

"He wouldn't share the bill with me, but I made him promise to let me pay next time."

"That's good. I'm glad to hear it, sweetheart."

Brendan wasn't the reason I had wanted to talk to Mum, and I wasn't looking forward to asking her about the things I needed to ask. No time like the present, though.

"So, Mum, I was wondering about a couple of things. And promise me you won't freak out."

"Ok?" The warmth of her voice subsided slightly, her scepticism coming through quite clearly.

"Well, Charlie and I, we're doing some research for a story I'm working on for the Whisper, and we happened to stumble upon a few things. Have you ever heard of the Harvester Academy?"

Seconds went by in complete silence before she exhaled sharply. "I have. Ruby, you have to promise me not to dig any deeper into the Academy!"

"But, Mum."

"They have ways of tracking people—Magicals—that would make your skin crawl. If you get on their radar, they will find you."

There was an edge of terror in the way she spoke. This was more than a little fear about dealers or the common Harvester on the street. This Academy sounded like it frightened her more than anything. I had never heard her this scared in my life.

"Sounds bad," I said.

"It is. Listen, the Academy recruits and trains Harvesters. They keep a low profile, and when you're recruited, you're not allowed to leave. They are ruthless. Killers of the worst kind, and highly organized.

Silence ensued. It sounded like Mum was holding her breath. After a while, I heard her sigh heavily.

"Now, I've told you all I can. Promise me you'll stop digging into this."

Not sure if that was a promise I could keep, but I had to calm her down. "I promise."

"Good. Now, you said there was something else?"

I hesitated. Mentioning the Harvester Academy hadn't been well received. Still, I was already head deep as it was.

"I did, yes. We also discovered something else while we were researching. There's a new drug on the market. The magical kind. They're calling it PureX. Ever heard of it?"

Mum scoffed. "It's not that new. That atrocity has been known for a few years. Problem is, they need pure-blooded Magicals to manufacture the drug, and we are one in ten thousand, maybe even fewer than that."

"But they are getting to it, though. There was mention of a vial sold for millions of pounds."

Mum paused again. "Likely a rare occurrence, though I'll do some digging to see what I can find out. There aren't a lot of us Pure Bloods left. You, however, should find yourself a different topic for your article. What on earth are you writing about anyway, that brings you close to this atrocity?"

Stupid, Ru. Why hadn't I come up with a fully fledged cover story before I rang Mum?

"Uhm, it's an article on drug addiction. Not the magical kind, though we accidentally stumbled upon it on the dark web."

Shut your trap, Ru. My big mouth always got me in

trouble. I hadn't needed to say anything about the dark web at all.

"Is that so? And how, pray tell, did you find yourself in the darkest corners of the internet?"

Mum was suspicious, and with good reason, but this was all I wanted to share with her for now. I couldn't have her worry about all the strange things that had been going on.

"Charlie is a computer whiz. We were tracking some names on suspected truckers, transporting pills, and Charlie dug as deep as she could, which is when we came across the magic marketplace."

Holy Lady of the Lake. I really put my foot in it this time.

"Ruby Guinevere Morgan! You stay away from places like that, you hear me?"

"Mum, I had to hold my phone at arm's length." I tried to laugh a little, but she didn't react. "Yes, sorry, I hear you."

"They could trace your address or maybe even your computer, making you a target yourself. You promised me you'd be careful, and this, young lady, is a far cry from being careful."

"I know, and I'm sorry. It won't happen again."

"It had better not."

We said our goodbyes quickly after that. Mum was furious, and with good reason. I couldn't bear to listen to her anger for another minute, however. Sure, I knew it was dangerous, but she couldn't stop me from digging deeper.

My earlier euphoria had drained completely and a pang of guilt settled in my stomach. I had lied to her again, good intentions or not, but I wasn't a baby anymore. Not only did I want to find out what had happened to Liv and Corinne, but I also needed to find out what had really happened to Dad. Something told me I was getting closer.

17

THE SOUND OF WAILING SIRENS MADE ME JUMP, MY PHONE falling from my lap to the floor. I picked it up and noticed the small crack on the screen just as Charlie came into the room. "I don't want to go full Luke Skywalker," she said, "but I've got a bad feeling about this."

"Me too," I said, looking out the window. "I can't see any police cars from here, but it sounded close. On campus kind of close."

"Let's go," she said.

We went outside, the chilly afternoon air nipping my skin, and sure enough, a steady flow of students moved in the same direction. I noticed the punk rocker from the altercation with Charlie at Freshers', hand in hand with what I assumed was "her man". Two guys ran past us, almost clipping my shoulder.

"I heard she was dehydrated," one said to the other.

"It's exsanguinated," the other replied. "When they drain the blood out of you."

My heart jumped at his words, and as we joined the flow of people, I sensed I would learn something horrible in a few minutes.

Near the southernmost end of campus, four identical three-storey, redbrick buildings surrounded a small square. In the middle stood a statue of a man on a horse, some thirty feet tall. I seemed to remember having read something on the uni app about that man being one of the founders of the university.

A crowd had already gathered, but they were kept out of the square by a line of yellow police tape. I spotted at least five officers, none of them Fernsby or Paddock, guarding the perimeter and telling people to stand back. Charlie and I worked our way through the crowd. That is, Charlie worked her way, and I tagged along as close as I could, saying "sorry" left and right. It was effective, however, and we eventually stood by the tape, looking at the scene.

The crime scene, as it were. Three police cars were parked in front of one of the buildings, and more police officers were busy raising a dark green tent behind the cars. Two men dressed in white hooded suits, blue gloves and blue shoe covers carried a large metal chest from the back of one of the cars and into the half-raised tent. Next to the tent stood our good cop/bad cop acquaintances from before. PC Fernsby held his phone to his ear, while PC Paddock scanned the crowd with an intense glare.

"It's a girl," said a voice to my right.

"Two girls, I heard," said another next to the first one.

"It has to be Corinne and Liv," I whispered to Charlie. "This is awful."

Charlie nodded. "Hang on, I've got an idea." She bent under the tape and walked towards one of the policemen guarding the scene.

"Hey! Stop there, young lady!" The police officer came running at her.

"Excuse me, Officer," Charlie said. "I may know who the victims are, if that is of any help?"

"There's only one victim. Now get back behind the tape, or I'll have to cuff you."

"I think I know them, I said," Charlie insisted.

"You don't," said the policeman. "And it's not *them*. It's a girl. Now get going, ok?"

"I will, sorry."

By the look on her face, I could tell she was split between the joy of having drawn the information from the copper and the fear of who the girl was. It could only be either Corinne or Liv, surely.

"Let's get out of here," Charlie said. "We can't do anything here, and we need to find Dunc."

I nodded, and we worked our way back through the crowd again—much easier going back than in. Charlie picked up her phone and tapped the screen a few times before holding it to her ear.

"Dunc? Where are you?" She looked at me, mouthing Old Willow. "Stay there until Ruby and I get there, all right? No, I don't—yes, I know. Stay put!"

We picked up the pace, and soon we were running towards the pub. When we entered, only three students sat at one of the window tables, and one by the bar— Duncan. The majority of students were probably at the crime scene. Charlie grabbed Duncan by the arm and dragged him to a table back in the corner by the toilets.

"Is it Liv?" she said with a low but panicky voice.

"What?" Duncan said.

"You don't know? The police are here, by the Founders' Square. Seems a girl is—" She looked at me with tears in her eyes. "They've found a girl, one of the coppers said."

"Oh," Duncan said. "I didn't think—were those sirens on campus?"

"What the hell is wrong with you?" I asked, anger stirring inside me. "Yes, the police are here, and I'm starting to wonder what you're not telling us. Do you know where Liv is, after all?"

His eyes were full of fear and confusion when he turned to me. "No! I just came here to—I don't know. Breathe for a few minutes. It's been hell inside my head since she disappeared."

I wanted to touch him so I could maybe tap into some of his memories but decided against it. He looked like he wanted to tell us something, so I tried another approach instead.

"You do know something, Dunc. And I believe you when you say you don't know where she is. But you know *what* she is, don't you?"

He sighed heavily, dropping his gaze to the table. Then his head started bobbing up and down, ever so slowly. "She had to run away. They caught her twice already, but she managed to escape. Her whole family is—"

He looked back up at me, then at Charlie, then back at me.

"They're gone," he said under his breath. "She told me a whole bunch of Harvesters came to the house one night. Her father tried to fight them but got slaughtered in front of his wife and daughters. Her mother started screaming, so one of the bastards jammed a knife straight through her throat."

I swallowed, tears swelling in my eyes as Charlie took Duncan's hands. He sniffled. "Liv and her sister, Violeta, were captured and taken to a dirty warehouse on the outskirts of Sofia, in Bulgaria. They're Banshees."

"Oh, crap," said Charlie. "That's why her mother screamed, right? They sense the death of family members or someone close, I think."

I nodded. "They're sort of cousins of—" I almost said *us*. "Of the Fae kind of Mags. I'm so sorry, Duncan. She came here to escape, is that it?"

"Yeah. Much good that did her." He shook his head. "The warehouse was a Mag farm, but not a very sophisticated or modern one. She and her sister were tied to some pipes by a brick wall and left in the dark for two days without food or water. The Harvesters were not exactly like the professionals in England, which was both good and bad for Liv. One day, two of the Harvesters went away, leaving only one to guard the Mags. He was an idiot according to Liv, so she managed to overpower and kill him. When the others returned, Liv killed one of them and escaped with her sister. Problem was, her sister was already badly hurt, and died in the woods outside the warehouse."

My blood had started to heat up as he spoke. I wasn't going to defend the level of professionalism on "our" Harvesters, but still. I pictured poor Liv and her mum in those dirty surroundings, having just watched their two closest family members being killed. Smoke started to rise from one of my hands, and I had to focus hard to stop the fire from escaping. I glanced at Charlie, who reacted quickly.

"Listen, Duncan," she said, dumping her jacket over my hands and grabbing him by the arm again. "Let's go back home and figure out what to do next."

She all but dragged him to the door. I stood to follow them but stopped when I saw the imprint of my palm burned onto the table surface. No one seemed to notice, though. I placed the little basket with spices and condiments over the burn mark and ran to catch up with the others.

Back in our flat, Duncan told us how Liv had escaped the Harvesters a third time, fighting off two of them with her bare hands. The young woman I saw swaying drunkenly at the party a few days ago had more fight in her than met the eye, it would seem. Not very typical of the peaceful Banshees, though.

"So, she hopped on a train and managed to sneak all the way to Paris, through a series of cargo carts. When she got there, she hitchhiked her way to Calais, and then through the Chunnel to England."

A knock on the door stopped him. He jumped to his feet. "They're going to think I killed her."

"They're not, Duncan," I said, not particularly convincing to either myself or him. "Besides, we don't know for sure the girl at the crime scene is Liv."

The people outside knocked again. "Miss Morgan?" a voice called. "Police, please open the door."

Duncan looked at me, pleadingly. "I wasn't here," he said and ran to Charlie's room.

I looked at Charlie, who shrugged. "We have to answer," she whispered.

Slowly, I moved towards the door, hoping to give Duncan enough time to climb out the window, which was what I presumed he would do.

"Police," the voice repeated, more intensely. "Open the—"

"I'm sorry," I said, opening the door. "I was listening to music." I tapped my ear to indicate I had been wearing my headset. "What's this about, Officer?"

"May I come in?" the officer said, and I stepped aside to let him. "I'm Detective Chief Inspector Davies. Are you Ruby Morgan?"

"Yes, I am. And this is my flatmate, Charlotte Hargraves."

Charlie stood by the couch, smiling as if nothing was wrong.

"How may we help you, Inspector?" I said.

Before I could close the door behind him, Officers Fernsby and Paddock entered. I hadn't noticed them behind him on the step outside. Fernsby nodded at me, a hint of sympathy in his eyes, while Paddock shot me a glance like the ones he had given me earlier, cold and judging.

Charlie gestured at the policemen to sit by the dinner table. "I'm sorry, but I don't think we have any tea prepared," she said.

DCI Davies raised his hand. "No, please. We have some questions, that's all."

He sat on the chair across the table from Charlie, and

I joined her on her side. Fernsby and Paddock remained standing behind the DCI.

"As you may or may not have heard, the police have secured a location on campus. It is, I'm sorry to say, the scene of a serious crime. Even though our crime scene investigators have yet to complete their work, we can confirm that a young woman has been found dead."

I drew in a breath. *Please don't let it be her!*

"Witnesses have confirmed it is the missing woman, the one who was here with false papers." He looked down on his notepad. "Ilyana Makarova."

"Oh, the poor girl," Charlie said. "She was supposed to be safe here."

"How well did you know her?" Davies asked.

"Not well at all," I replied. "She is a—was a friend of Duncan's. They were close friends. He helped her."

"Helped her with what, exactly?"

I decided the only way now was the truth, and even if that would send the police in Duncan's direction, I had to let the DCI know about Liv. And I also decided to stop calling her that. A small gesture of respect, perhaps.

"Ilyana lost her whole family to a group of blood Harvesters in her home town in Bulgaria. She barely managed to escape, only to find her so-called haven here in London to be the exact same kind of hellhole she left."

Again, the mere thought of Harvesters roaming campus looking for—and killing—Magicals, ignited the fire in me. I took another few deep breaths, and it seemed to help quell the flames I could feel slinking underneath my skin. "Duncan's only crime is that he helped a refugee, one society viewed as illegal, both as an immigrant and as a Magical."

"What crime has and has not been committed is a bit premature to decide, Miss Morgan, but I understand your sentiment," DCI Davies said. "Where is Duncan now?"

"Dunno," Charlie said, touching my knee under the table. "My guess is he's exactly where he's been the last few days. Out looking for his friend."

"Right," Paddock scoffed. "Looking for his next victim, more like it."

"That will be all, PC Paddock," Davies said, his voice a gunshot. "Report to the scene. Crowd control."

"Sir?" Paddock sighed.

"Now, PC Paddock!"

Even with the thought of Ilyana lying dead in that dark tent, I had to suppress a smile.

"Have you seen Duncan today, ladies?" Davies continued.

"No, sir. I've been in my room all day, studying. I just came out to ask Ruby if we should get something to eat when you knocked on the door."

That was a big risk, and I think she knew it. At least four people at the Old Willow saw us with Duncan there, and maybe more had seen us walking back here together. Still, everyone was busy talking about or running towards the crime scene, so maybe they hadn't paid attention to us.

"I see. When was the last time you saw him?"

"Not sure," I said. "Sometime last night, perhaps? Lectures have started, and my head is a mess trying to keep up. It's not quite the laid-back pace of upper secondary."

It wasn't exactly a lie as my head really was a mess,

even if it had nothing to do with the introductory lessons.

"I can imagine," Davies said. "Still, we have a serious situation here, and will need to speak to Duncan as soon as possible."

"Have you tried his phone, perhaps?" Charlie said innocently.

"Yes, we have, Miss Hargraves. To no avail, I'm sorry to say. Maybe he will answer if you call him?"

Charlie pulled out her phone, but before she managed to dial, DCI Davies lay his hand across the table. "Put it on speaker, please."

My pulse was racing. The fire, however, was nowhere to be felt. This was just pure anxiousness.

Charlie did as the detective ordered, and soon we heard the ring tone. Once. Twice. After the sixth ring, Dunc's voice came through the speaker. "Hey! You know exactly who this is, seeing as you've called me. Leave a message, and make it interesting, so I may find it worth my time to call you back. Cheers."

Davies nodded at Charlie, who leaned her head over the mic.

"Hi, Dunc. It's me, your fave roomie. Give me a call as soon as you get this. It's important."

She tapped the red icon to hang up, looking across at the DCI.

"Were any of you aware of Miss Makarova's heritage?" he said, looking back and forth between us.

"Her heritage?" I asked. "That she was a Banshee, you mean? Yes, Duncan told us."

"When?"

"Not sure, really," I lied. "Yesterday or maybe earlier.

He made no secret of it after she disappeared. It was why she was here, fleeing the—" I wanted to say farm, but I had no idea what Duncan had meant by it. "A warehouse in Sofia."

I had to ask Mum about Mag farms. The term alone gave me the creeps.

"I will level with you, ladies. The woman, Miss Makarova, was indeed a Magical. And yes, we believe the technical term is Banshee. As you may know, those are not the most sought-after Magicals on the MagX scene. Not the, how shall I say, sexiest of powers. I believe the term was on Jeremy Kyle the other night."

My stomach churned, and not only because the policeman watched that sickening show.

"The *sexiest* of powers," I repeated, shaking my head. "That is such a racist way of putting it. I get that MagX has some qualities, drug-like qualities, that appeal to a certain group of people."

I felt bad for Charlie but didn't want to sugar-coat my words anymore. "But I hate that it does, and I hate that it's being talked about in such terms. Like it's fun for a Magical to get her blood drained and sold as a bloody novelty."

Charlie kicked me under the table, but I ignored her. She just had to take it, I thought.

"I agree," Davies said. "MagX is illegal, and so far that's the only part of the magical society that is. I am aware of the proposals from some of the more right-wing politicians, banning Magicals altogether, but I can assure you the London police are on the same page as you, Miss Morgan."

His words took me by surprise. "What do you mean?"

"Even if the media likes to portray us as hitting down on Magicals, especially those who use their powers for criminal purposes, we have a policy—one that comes from the very top of the judicial branches of government, I might add. It clearly states that Magicals and humans are equal in the eyes of the law, and that is what guides us in our daily work. Frankly, I am willing to bet that is also the mindset of the thousands of policemen and women across the country."

I noticed Fernsby shifting his feet behind the detective. Somehow I believed Davies, but I was not convinced he had the whole force on his side in the matter.

"Right now, however, we do have a serious crime to investigate."

"You mean she was murdered, don't you?" I said, looking into his eyes.

"I cannot comment on the nature of the crime at this stage, Miss Morgan, as I am sure you understand. You're studying to become a journalist, are you not?"

"Yes," I said, not sure why that mattered one way or the other.

"And back home in Cheshire, you have already published several pieces in the local newspaper about Magicals and the illegal blood market." Not asking as much as stating a fact this time.

"That's correct."

"Then I'm sure you will be very familiar with sharing important information with the authorities. Please continue that tradition, and contact me as soon as you, or your friend here, think of something—anything—that might have to do with this matter. Even if it seems minute or unimportant."

He lay two business cards on the table next to Charlie's phone and stood to leave, PC Fernsby in tow. As they reached the door, I walked towards him, holding out my hand. He looked at it, puzzled, but took it.

"Thank you, DCI Davies," I said. "We'll call if we hear or see something."

When the door closed behind them, I slid to the floor. Charlie came running over, crouching next to me.

"What is it, Ru?"

"They—they—" I sobbed, the image from DCI Davies' thoughts burning in my head. "They drained all her blood, Char!"

18

CHARLIE AND I WERE BOTH REELING WITH WHAT FELT LIKE A bad hangover from the day before. I had half slept through my second day of lectures, while Charlie hadn't even been to hers, and now I was bunked on a heap of pillows beside her bed again, both of us exhausted.

Jen, however, wasn't in the same sorry state we were. She stood in the doorway, tilting her head at us.

"Jeez, you guys are no fun at all today. Are you going to crawl out from under all that misery any time soon?"

"Nope," Charlie replied, her voice muffled by the pillow hugging her face.

"Red?"

"Not today, Jen. I'm beat," I mumbled.

"Fine." Jen put her hands on her hips. "I'll go to Diane on my own. We're taking pictures for my Insta." She practically scowled at us. "My audience isn't interested in sad faces like yours anyway. I'll see you both once you look like my friends again."

She turned on her heels and disappeared down the hallway, the front door slamming shut.

"What's her beef?" I asked Charlie.

"She thinks it's a waste of time—you know, wallowing like we're doing right now. None of us actually knew Ilyana. Besides, I think Jen's scared, even if she doesn't show it. Someone killed Ilyana, and whoever did it is still walking around free." She lifted her head an inch. "Maybe she's right. We should get off our sorry arses and do something useful."

"Maybe."

We stayed there a couple of hours longer until Charlie decided she was over it.

"Can't waste an entire day, I suppose. Not when there's someone out there killing Mags." She looked down at me with beady eyes. "What if they know about you?"

The thought had more than crossed my mind, especially after what had happened at the Halfway, though I couldn't be sure if that incident and what happened to those girls had anything to do with one another. The thought did make me shiver, and Mum's words of caution whispered in my head.

"They don't," I said, trying to sound confident.

Charlie dangled her feet over the edge of the bed, her toes a little too close to my face, forcing me to sit.

"I figured you out on day one," she said. "Who's to say I'm the only one who realized what you did and what you are?"

"I guess we're back to our 'needle in a stack of bigger needles' hunt, then?"

"You bet."

I tied the nest that was my hair into a loose bun, and we went back to our previous search on the magic market. And though Mum's words were gnawing at the back of my mind, I couldn't keep my promise to her. Not now.

Charlie typed in a few of the names and words from the page we came across on our last search: *MagX swapping, Cheap MagX* and so on, but only got to the same ads.

One search, *Camelot Inc.,* sent us to a series of firewalls and protected sites within other protected sites. Charlie tried to get past them but had to give up.

I sighed. "We're not going to get anywhere with this."

"Then we find a different approach."

"Like what?"

Charlie scooted her chair back, adjusting her glasses. "I know who Dunc's dealer is. And where there are dealers, Harvesters won't be far behind."

I frowned. "What do you mean, you know who his dealer is?"

"Her name is Shauna." Charlie wavered, fidgeting with her phone. "I have her number."

"Oh," I muttered as I realized the connection.

"Yeah—I haven't been in contact with her since Diane's party, I promise, though I can text her and ask if she can meet us for an exchange."

The thought of Charlie anywhere near that dealer made my fists ball up. I didn't need her falling back into that rabbit hole.

"As long as you promise me you'll delete her number once we've talked to her."

"Scout's honour." Charlie placed three fingers to her temple.

"You've never been a scout a day in your life, have you?" I laughed softly.

"Nope." Charlie grinned. "Guess you'll just have to take my word for it. I'll text her now."

While we waited for a reply, my mind drifted. I didn't want to ask, but I couldn't keep it to myself anymore. "Are we sure Dunc doesn't have anything to do with Ilyana's death?"

"A couple of days ago, I would have said yes. Now, I honestly don't know."

"I don't either."

"Let's give him the benefit of the doubt," Charlie said, "and see what we can find out."

"Totally."

It didn't take long before Shauna answered Charlie's text.

Fifteen. The labyrinth.

"Where?"

"Have you not seen the labyrinth garden yet? Come on."

I shook my head, and Charlie grabbed my hand, yanking me out of our flat.

We passed the lecture hall where I had spent my morning and ended up at a part of campus I hadn't seen so far. A large fountain stood in the middle of a square, surrounded by still-blooming flowers and evergreens. Charlie guided me past it and into what looked like it might well be a never-ending labyrinth of tall hedges.

I stopped in my tracks, letting go of Charlie's hand. "You sure you know how to get out of there?"

"Of course I do." She took my hand again. "We're not going far, just far enough so no one will see us."

We entered into the labyrinth and pushed ourselves through a hedge wall, where people had been in and out before, judging by the broken twigs and bent stems. A twig stuck in my hair.

"We're here," Charlie said.

I looked around. The walls of the labyrinth were taller here, and I couldn't pinpoint an exact exit. The area was spacious, shaped like a square, and a metal bench stood by the hedgerow at the far end of what almost felt like a glade in a forest. I ran a hand through my hair and stopped as my fingers caught hold of the twig. I couldn't get it out.

"Do you mind?" I asked Charlie, pointing to my head.

She laughed, and we went to sit on the bench where she spent a whole five minutes untangling the twig. Not that we didn't have time. It took another thirty before Shauna entered from the same spot we had. Her thick, springy hair gathered more leaves and branches than mine had. She shook her hair free of what she could and let the rest stay where it was.

Shauna faced us and eyed me warily. "Who's the tag-along?" she called.

"She's cool," Charlie said.

"Is she buying?" Shauna came closer, closing the gap between us.

"Actually," I interjected, standing to meet her, "we're not buying anything today. Sorry about that. We kind of just had to ask you a question."

"I'm out." Shauna turned away, but I couldn't let her leave.

My blood ran hot, simmering in my veins as my magic flared through me. The surge of power ricocheted through my blood, willing itself to break free. I opened my hands and shot out what was meant to be a force field. Instead, a rush of flames blasted through the air to form a ring of fire around Shauna. Sweat immediately coated her brow as she turned back, staring at me with blatant dread in her dark brown eyes.

"What is this?" Shauna howled. "Don't hurt me!"

I cupped my hands and a set of fireballs formed in my palms while I stepped closer. "As I said, we have a question."

Charlie grabbed my forearm and I shot her a cold look, making her back up.

"Who supplies the blood you're dealing?" I asked Shauna, not quite recognizing my voice.

A flame licked past a lock of her curly black hair, singeing it at the edges. "Please. Stop!" she cried.

"Who supplies the drugs?" I pressed.

"Greg," she shouted. "His name is Greg."

"Ru! Let her go!" Charlie's voice was shaky but determined. She grabbed my arm again, and my head snapped to look at her. "Girl, your eyes. Let Shauna go. Now!"

I struggled against myself. Part of me wanted to let the flames have their way; they begged me to allow them to devour Shauna. But Charlie begged me not to. The fear was written all over my friend's face. I pulled air into my lungs, focusing on the only thing I could, the purest part of myself, my healing power. Spirals of shimmering white wisps wrapped around the fireballs, dancing outwards to shift around the ring of fire. The flames died down, shooting back into my blood along with the wisps of white. They moved inside me, raging against one another until I closed my hands and commanded them to still with my mind. My blood stopped simmering, and I staggered backwards, heaving for breath.

Shauna shifted her weight, swaying on her feet for a moment, then darted away from me faster than I thought she was able to before crashing through the hedge to disappear from sight.

I slumped to the ground, my eyes locked on the circle of singed grass in front of me. What the hell had I done?

"Ruby?" Charlie prompted, crouching in front of me. "Are you with me, love?"

"I—I'm here."

"What the fudge happened? I knew you had some heat in there, but I didn't know you could shoot actual fire from your hands."

"Neither did I until the last few days," I admitted.

"I thought you said Fae didn't have those kinds of powers?" She tilted her head at me, looking every bit as confused as I was myself.

I was shaking, trembling into a ball. "They don't. *We* don't."

I couldn't wrap my head around it, so I couldn't exactly expect Charlie to understand it any more than I did.

"At least we got a name," I said, hunching my shoulders.

Charlie narrowed her gaze at me. "That was some scary shit, Ru."

"Tell me you're not scared of me. Please. I didn't mean to. Do you hate me now?"

Was this it? Was this the moment when I lost the one person I thought could be my friend for life? I couldn't blame her if she wanted to run for the hills, but I needed her to stay.

"It freaked me out, I'm not gonna lie, but I could never hate you, pumpkin. You're my friend, and whatever the heck is happening inside you, we'll figure it out. Together."

She folded her arms around me, pulling me into a hug. "Let's focus on this Greg for now, though. If you're up for it?"

I hugged her back, squeezing tight. The fact that Charlie didn't shy away from me, even now, made my heart expand with hope.

"I'm up for it. I think. Thank you, Charlie. I don't know what would have happened if you hadn't been here."

"That's my job, silly. As your friend and all. For better or worse and all that." She gave me a hand, helping me to my feet, then wrapped her pinkie with mine. "Friends for life, Ru Ru."

I nodded.

"Let's find this Greg, then."

"You know who he is?" I asked.

"Nope. Not heard of him. I know a lot of people, but there are hundreds of students on campus. I'm not exactly a walking student roster, but I can always fish one out for us."

We returned to Charlie's room, and within minutes, she had hacked her way into the university server.

"They really ought to get better firewalls," said Charlie, her voice back to its normal chipper tone. "Let's see if anyone is named Greg, shall we?" She typed in the name, and twelve results popped up.

"Guess we're excluding people first, then see who we're left with?" I asked.

"Good call. There's a lecturer called Greg." Charlie snickered. "Man, he looks ancient. I think it's safe to assume that this guy is not fit to be a Harvester."

"Talk about fit." I pointed at another name on the list. "Harvesters probably need to be well trained. That guy is too heavy, I think."

"Agreed."

We went down the list, and could easily exclude everyone who didn't look like they enjoyed going to the gym on a regular basis. In the end, we were left with only three names.

"Uh, Ru." Charlie nudged a finger to a picture on the screen. "Recognize him?"

I gasped as I recognized his face. "The janitor?"

"The janitor, aka Greg Barrows," Charlie confirmed.

I stood for a moment, transfixed by the prospect. We did have two other candidates on the list, and we couldn't be a hundred percent certain that the Greg we were looking for was even on this roster. Still, my intuition told me we had our guy. At least he was *a* guy, of the Harvester kind. I was almost sure of it.

"Should we tell Jen?"

Charlie scratched her ear. "She's with Diane. If we're wrong, then it would be very uncool to accuse the guy she likes. Let's dig a little deeper and tell her once we know more."

Not sure if it was a good idea or not, I agreed.

"How do you know where to look for all this?" I asked. "Aren't these things kept secure?"

"There's secure, and then there's secure," she said. "You'd be surprised to see how many government and public services data systems are as open as Tescos. At least to someone like me."

It didn't take long before she had half a dozen windows open on her computer—adoption records and child protective services among others. She searched for any records she could find on our suspect janitor. The pieces seemed to match up. There was no record of him, nothing at all to be found between the age of fifteen and the age of twenty. It was as if he hadn't existed at all during those five years. He was an orphan, raised within the system, bouncing from one family to another.

"Crap on a cracker," Charlie exclaimed. "When he was fourteen, his foster parents went missing. They were never found."

"That's it. I'm calling Jen." I pressed the dial button and listened to the sound of the ring tone. No answer. "You try," I said to Charlie.

She placed the phone to her ear and waited. "Not picking up. She's probably mid-shoot. We'll tell her when she gets back."

I turned to the screen again, Greg Barrows leering back at me. This creep had been right under my nose since the day I arrived, and all I had seen was a handsome guy, someone who changed the lightbulbs and helped people fix their sinks and whatnots. The phrase *looks can be deceiving* sprang to mind. I would not make that mistake again. We couldn't be sure if Greg had anything to do with Liv or Corinne, but I was sure about one thing as I stared at him now—this guy was a Harvester.

We're on to you, bloodsucker.

19

I TOOK A FINAL LOOK INTO MY SHOULDER BAG TO MAKE sure I had brought extra pens and a notebook as well as a charger and my laptop, which was all I needed for a lecture on source criticism. Placing the bag over my shoulder, I stepped into the hallway and hurried to the front door. I only had ten minutes to get to the lecture hall, and this was one I hadn't been to yet.

"Ru," Charlie called after me. "Wait up."

"I need to run or I'll be late."

She caught up with me, and a sense of worry built in my chest.

"What?" I asked. "What's wrong?"

"Jen didn't come home last night, and she's not been back in her room."

My heart sank like a stone through water, and I put a hand on the wall to steady myself. "Have you tried calling her? Or Diane?"

"Both go straight to voicemail," Charlie murmured. "I'm worried something might have happened. What if someone snatched her on the way home last night? What if—"

"Don't think like that," I cut her off. "They probably had a few drinks, and Jen is sleeping it off back at Raven Court. Plus, the other girls, Liv and Corinne, were Magicals. Jen isn't. I'm sure she's fine. Even if she is dating a Harvester scumbag."

"You're probably right." Charlie relaxed her shoulders. "Go on then. I don't have any lectures today, so I'll go to Diane's and check on Jen."

I hesitated. "Sure? I could come with you?"

"Nah. You have studies. Go. I'll text you when I find her."

I didn't want her to go on her own, but Mum would kill me if I began ditching classes before I had even started them. "Text me as soon as you know, all right?"

"Will do."

I sprinted out the door and found the lecture hall five minutes too late. Lucky for me, it hadn't started yet. The students were still murmuring amongst themselves, while the lecturer was having a technical argument with the sound equipment. I snuck in and found a seat on the back row. A guy further to the front stood to help the lecturer with his tech.

"Thank you, Frank." The lecturer's voice boomed through the speakers before he turned the sound down to a more pleasing level. "Now, my name is Míng Jié Zhang, but you may refer to me as Mr Zhang."

There was only a hint of his Chinese heritage in his otherwise nearly perfect British. Silver strands ran through his long black hair, which was combed back over his head, falling just above his shoulders.

"This is your first lecture on journalistic criticism. It is important that you understand the ramifications of not verifying your sources, and in this day and age, it's especially difficult to navigate truth from deception."

A slide appeared on the large screen at the front as Mr Zhang dove into his lecture. It was interesting enough, and I wanted to pay more attention, but my mind kept drifting back to Jen, and our recent discovery on the janitor's spare-time activities. It didn't sit well with me, knowing that he was a Harvester and that he was dating Jen, though I figured he wouldn't harm her as long as she was just a normal human. Maybe he really liked her?

I retrieved my phone, hiding it behind the screen of my laptop while texting Charlie.

Anything yet?

Seconds later, my phone vibrated with a reply.

Nothing. She's not at Raven, followed by a sad smiley.

My finger slid over the screen, texting my response.

Ok. Meet you back at Craydon after class?

Charlie sent me a thumbs up, and I raised my head to the presentation again, a growing pit of worry settling heavily in my gut. The one and a half hours were starting to feel more like an entire day as the lecture continued. I needed to get out of there. It was as if my blood was expanding in my veins, tugging at me to leave.

Something was definitely up.

"Think about it. That would be all for today," Mr Zhang announced, making me bounce out of my seat. "Make sure you check for your assignment. It will be posted on the LMS later today." His voice faded in the background as I dashed outside and back to the flat.

"Charlie?" I called as I ran through the front door to her room. It was empty. I dropped my bag on her bed. "Char?" I cried out.

"In here," Charlie replied from across the hall.

I walked over and shifted my eyes around Jen's room. The usually tidy space was cluttered with her stuff, and Charlie was the obvious culprit behind the mess. She was turning everything over, darting back and forth like a chipmunk.

"Jen is not going to like this," I mumbled.

"Well, when she goes off like this, staying out after curfew, and doesn't even let us know where she is, she can only blame herself," Charlie said in a rush before kneeling by Jen's bed, sticking her head underneath it. Moments later, she crawled back out with a wooden box in her hands. It looked handcrafted from gorgeous ebony wood, with a moon carved out on the lid, a sapphire gleaming on each corner.

She stroked a hand over the box. "I'm so worried about her, is all." Her fingers touched the clasp on the front. "Should we open it?"

"Not sure what other choices we have." I sat next to her on the floor. "She would understand, I think."

Together, we unhinged the clasp and lifted the lid off the box to take a look inside.

The box was filled with pictures of what I assumed was Jen's family, their features undeniably similar. A man, a woman, and four other children in addition to Jen were immortalized in the pictures. One of them had the entire family gathered on a mountainside somewhere. I didn't recognize the place, but it was probably the Alps or someplace similar.

"I had no idea she has four siblings," I said.

"I know, right?" Charlie said, giving me a tired smile.

A necklace called out to me underneath the pile of pictures, and I brought the chain up between two fingers. A silver half-moon pendant embedded with three small sapphires dangled in front of my eyes. It was stunning.

"Ruby." Charlie nudged me in the side as she brought one of the pictures to my attention. "Is this what I think it is?"

Thick, white fur was the first thing to catch my attention of the wolf in the picture. It was taken in the same spot as the family portrait. Then I noticed the blue eyes. Even in wolf form, I would have recognized them anywhere. I sucked in a breath, recalling all the times I had seen those eyes lately.

My mind raced back to everything that had happened from the first day I arrived on campus. Jen always seemed to have a sixth sense about things, like she knew when to keep her distance, and when not to. She had literally sniffed her way to find the syringe outside Raven Court. Did she already know then that it contained human blood? The image of her parting the rose bush with her hands without getting scratched moved to the forefront of my memories. How had I not seen it before?

"It is," I replied. "Jen is a Shifter!"

20

THE FLAT SEEMED EMPTY WITH ONLY THE TWO OF US SITTING at the kitchen table. With Duncan and Jen missing, it was just Charlie and me left.

"Should we inform the police?" Charlie asked, almost inaudibly.

"It didn't exactly turn out great the last time we neglected to tell them about a missing girl, did it?"

"Guess not." Charlie sighed deeply. "Those coppers, though. I have absolutely no desire to speak to Paddock again. He creeps me out."

He creeped me out too. A lot. Still, I had learned from my previous mistake, and I had no intention of being thrown in the nick, as Paddock so kindly put it. I brought my phone up and found PC Paddock's number. I wished I had Fernsby's number instead, but this was the number we had been provided with. I dialled, switched to the speaker, and put the phone at the centre of the table.

He answered on the fifth ring. "Paddock."

"Hi, this is Ruby Morgan, at White Willow University. You remember me?"

"I do. What are you up to this time?"

I blew into my hair and braced myself for what I had to say. "I'm just—I'm calling to tell you that our flatmate, Jeannine Lune, has gone missing. She didn't come home last night, and we haven't seen her since."

Paddock went very quiet at the other end before he spoke again. "And how many hours since you saw her last, Miss Morgan?"

I gestured at Charlie, opening my hands as a question. She shrugged and showed me ten fingers, then four.

"About fourteen hours," I told Paddock.

"Well, then, I wouldn't worry too much, Miss Morgan. She's probably sleeping off a party at a friend's, or maybe a boyfriend's."

"She's not—" I began.

"Listen, I'll put a flag in our system about it, and check if we have someone to send over, ok? Let me know if she shows up in the meantime. If not, you contact me again, and we'll open an investigation."

"What?" I blurted. "She could be dead somewhere." Taking a deep breath, I held back the curse words I wanted to shout at him, then continued in a more gentle tone. "I mean, why were you so hard on us the last time if you don't even want to look for her now?"

"Miss Morgan," he said, his voice like steel. "You are still to report something like this. If you haven't already, I would advise you to report it to the security guards on campus for the time being. I'll expect to hear back from you."

"All right. Thanks, I guess."

"Goodbye, Miss Morgan."

"Bye," I mumbled.

Charlie pushed back her chair and leapt to her feet. "Great." She started pacing the room. "Just what we needed."

What were we going to do now? The guards on campus were nice and all, but they hadn't exactly done a bang-up job finding the other missing girls, and Ilyana was already confirmed dead. Who else could we turn to?

"I've got an idea," I said, grabbing my phone again and sliding down to one of my most recent calls. It rang twice before he picked up. "Hey B," I said.

"Milady," Brendan replied, and my body relaxed at the sound of his voice.

"We need your help," I continued. "Jen is missing. Could you meet us by the white willow?"

Brendan didn't miss a beat. "I'll be down in a jiffy."

"You think he can help?" Charlie asked as we walked out of Craydon to meet him.

"Maybe. Worth a shot at least."

Brendan was already waiting for us beneath the shade of the willow, leaning on the trunk. God, he looked great. My heart was somersaulting at the sight of him. This isn't a romantic encounter, though, Ruby, I told myself, steadying my breathing.

"Howya, ladies," Brendan said.

"Thank you for meeting us." I gave him a quick hug, inhaling his spicy scent for a moment before stepping back. "We might have a lead."

I explained everything that had happened since Jen left the house the previous day, including our lead on

Greg Barrows, the janitor, but excluding the part about the wolf in the pictures. He didn't need to know what Jen was in order to help us look for her.

"Sounds to me like the janitor is our best clue. Let's go to the student information office. They'll know where he's accommodated. All the staff have their own accommodation on campus, so he shouldn't be too hard to find."

That was a good idea, but something was off with Brendan today. I couldn't quite put my finger on it. He did most of the talking as we walked to the information office, rambling on about everything and nothing, including some tournament he was attending in a few months. Charlie gave me a confused look, clearly picking up on that same weird vibe I was. Brendan was always confident, but I had never seen him go on as he did now.

"Here we are. You ladies can wait outside while I get what we need from Mrs Pryce. She knows me," he said and disappeared inside.

"What's up with him today?" Charlie asked.

I folded one hand over my arm. "No idea. He's not usually like this."

We didn't get a chance to talk more as Brendan dashed out of the door again. "Got it," he said. "Greg lives here. A seven-minute walk, give or take."

Our walk continued in the same fashion as before. Neither Charlie nor I could get more than a couple of words in during the one-sided conversation.

"Is that it?" Charlie interrupted, pointing down a steep stairwell, which led to a steel door on the sub-zero level. A sign on the wall read *Staff Accommodation*.

Brendan bounced down the steps. "Yup," he called. "Has his name on the door."

We followed down the stone steps while Brendan knocked. No answer.

"Guess no one is home," he said.

"Perfect." Charlie pulled a pin out of my hair, releasing a collection of locks to fall around my face. "We can take a look around, then."

"We can?" I said.

"Sure," Charlie replied and straightened the bobby pin. She put the tip of it into the lock and bent it downward, proceeding to curl one of the ends into a makeshift handle. With a broad smile, she held the finished product up in front of her face. "You learn a lot of tricks when your dad tends to lock your door—with you inside." She shrugged.

I wanted to wrap her in my arms and tell her everything was all right but didn't want to disturb her.

Charlie slid the newly made lock pick into the lock and started jiggling it gently up and down, then side to side. I gasped as the door clicked open.

"Coming?" Charlie asked.

I exchanged a look with Brendan, who stood back.

"I think I'll keep watch. You girls go ahead. Breaking and entering isn't really my style, though for this particular reason, I'm inclined to think that the ends justifies the means. But you'll excuse me if I don't wish to become your partner in real crime."

He gave me a peck on the cheek. "Keep your phone close, and I'll ring you if you need to get out fast."

"Thanks," I said, then followed Charlie inside.

Being so far below ground, the only natural light

inside came from four narrow windows close to the ceiling, leaving the room in a gloomy state. We stepped into what looked like a more or less normal living room with a sparse amount of furniture, then walked through to the kitchen. The rank smell of mould and old dishes hit me like a wall.

"Gross," Charlie uttered, covering her mouth with her hand until we entered the next room.

My jaw dropped. A table to my right was filled with blood vials, blood bags, panels—and several syringes. I lifted my gaze to the back wall, my heart racing like I was running a sprint.

"What the—" Charlie stepped over to the wall and pulled down a picture, showing it to me. "Ilyana." Her words were stifled.

I went to her side and took her hand. There were about a dozen more pictures of Ilyana next to a bunch of pictures that I recognized from the one Paddock had shown us of Corinne. Charlie's hand stiffened in my hold as we both looked at the twenty or so pictures of Jen. They had been taken all over campus, some blurrier than others—clearly shot with a zoom lens. Jen outside our house, behind the windows at Brady's, and even one in the darkness of our regular pub, the Old Willow. Barrows must have stalked her like a paparazzo.

"That bastard," she breathed before ripping every last one of them down, stuffing them into her jeans pockets.

A shiver crawled over my skin. "Charlie," I whispered. "Look."

She followed my line of sight to the pile of pictures on a chair by my side.

"Shit, Ru." She grabbed the lot of them. "He knows about you."

The words stuck in my throat, and I couldn't say anything. Greg the wannabe paparazzo had at least ten pictures of me too in that pile.

"We gotta get out of here," Charlie whispered.

She tugged me with her through the flat and back outside where she shoved the pictures of me into the back of her jeans. Then she covered her bulging pockets by tying her jumper around her waist before we climbed the steps to meet up with Brendan.

"Find anything?" he asked, taking me in his arms. "Hey, Ruby, you're shaking like a leaf."

"He has a wall full of pictures—of Olivia and Corinne," Charlie explained, keeping Jen and me out of the equation when I couldn't muster the words. "He's definitely our guy."

"Feck!" Brendan said.

"He—he killed Ilyana," I sobbed into Brendan's chest. "What if he killed Corinne, too, and—"

"Don't." Charlie cut me off. "Don't say her name."

Brendan stroked my hair. "Ilyana was missing for a while, so maybe she wasn't killed straight away. There could still be a window of time here."

It wasn't extremely encouraging, but he did have a point. I straightened, wiping my eyes. "Then there's no time to waste. We need to find her. Now!"

Charlie tilted her head at me, a veil of sadness coating her eyes, but neither of us was giving up on Jen.

"Time to call the police, don't you think?" Brendan asked.

"I did. They didn't exactly jump into action. Said she hasn't been gone long enough."

"But you've got more evidence now."

"Which we obtained by breaking and entering. Besides, I don't trust them," I admitted. "And the clock is ticking. What if they don't get here in time?"

And what if they realized the connection of Jen being a Mag? I couldn't tell Brendan that, but I didn't want to be the one to expose Jen as a shifter either.

"Excuse me," a male voice said. "Are you looking for someone."

We turned to face him, and Charlie was quick on her feet. "We're researching for a paper I'm doing on the architectural structures of White Willow," she said. "It's for one of my 'archaeology through history' lectures."

A part of me admired Charlie's ability to lie on the spot, but I wished she hadn't needed that skill to survive.

The man smiled at us and I remembered him from when he broke up the fight between Charlie and the punk girl. His outfit looked as outdated yet refined as the last time I had seen him. He had to be somewhere in his sixties, and there was something in his eyes that made me feel calm.

"I'm Professor Kaine, and it so happens that I know quite a lot about historical endeavours, architectural or otherwise. But if you need to dig deeper for other source material, I suppose I could lend you a hand and offer you access into the university archives at the library. You'll need a password." He winked at me.

"Not rea—I, mean, that would be awesome," Charlie said.

"Very well, then, just you follow me."

We did as asked and trailed behind him to the White Willow Grand Library. He took us through the main hall to the back, where he slid his key card in the reader, which opened the door to another room. Charlie's eyes widened, and I had to admit the room was impressive.

"This is where we keep the more special collections of books that need to be handled with the utmost care. There is another room with older books, too, but that one is out of bounds, and hardly a place you need to visit for what you're looking for," Professor Kaine said.

The circular room contained a row of six-storey, white wooden bookshelves covering the walls from one side to the other. In the middle of the room, however, was a more modern looking display, consisting of a large table with four stationary computers and adjacent chairs.

Professor Kaine sat down on one of them and turned the computer on, glancing at Brendan.

"Did I not see you by the lake with that pretty American girl the other night?" he asked. "What was her name again?"

"Uhm, maybe," Brendan replied.

"Yes, I'm quite sure of it. The two of you are an item, I suppose?" Kaine tilted his chin. "Ah, Diane, that was it."

My shoulders slumped and a tinge of the old green monster I had become familiar with wriggled in my bones. What had he been doing by the lake? With Diane, of all people.

Brendan scratched his jaw. "No, sir. Just a friend."

That was a relief. At the same time, what was he

supposed to say with me standing right next to him? Was she just a friend? Or was Brendan not the guy I thought he was? I bit down on my tongue, mentally shaking myself. I couldn't think about this right now. I had to focus on finding Jen.

"Oh, well," Professor Kaine replied, turning his attention to the computer. He typed his credentials, meticulously pressing one key at a time, then looked back to us. "There you are. There's a map section, and a registry on all the buildings on campus. Feel free to print the articles you need. My account is void of the limitations your student accounts have on printing. I'll give you some privacy and attend to some research of my own in the meantime." His eyes shifted around the room. Nodding, he went over to the bookcases, and the three of us began searching the archives.

"What exactly are we looking for?" Brendan pulled a finger along his collar.

"Well," Charlie said under her breath, "it stands to reason that the janitor would keep the girls somewhere on campus. All the girls disappeared from campus grounds, and Ilyana was found dead here. Then there are the disturbing things we found in Barrows' flat. I don't think he would risk transporting everything too far, so I'm guessing the girls never left the grounds."

I could almost kiss her. While I was a complete mess, Charlie managed to keep her wits about her and think clearly. It didn't take her long to dig into the map archives until she found what we needed.

"Here," she pointed at the screen. "It's a blueprint of every structure on the White Willow premises. See here?" Her finger slid across the map. "That's a tunnel system. And here at the end is an old boiler room that's been shut down."

I snapped a few pictures of the map, not wanting to wait to print it. "You're a freaking genius! Have I told you that before?"

"You have, but it doesn't hurt to repeat it." She smirked, then deleted her entire search history before shutting the computer off.

Kaine turned to us. "Find what you needed?" he asked.

"Yes, thank you, Professor," I said.

"Good. And Ruby—it is Ruby, right?"

"Yes." Had I given him my name? It appeared I had, though I couldn't remember doing it.

"Remember that people will do anything, no matter how absurd, in order to avoid facing their own souls. One does not become enlightened by imagining figures of light, but by making the darkness conscious."

"Uhm, ok," I said.

"Carl Jung?" Charlie asked.

"Indeed, Miss?"

"Medina Hargraves. I'm fine with Hargraves alone."

He nodded at her. "Hargraves it is, then."

"Ok," I said again, having no idea what he meant. "I'll try to remember that. And again, thank you for your help."

"Any time, Ruby." He waved us off and returned his attention to the books.

Finding our way back outside, we settled on a patch of grass to study the pictures of the blueprints more closely.

"What do you think, Brendan?" I asked, to no reply. I

shifted my head around, but there was no sight of Brendan anywhere. "What? Where did he go?"

Charlie shrugged. "Dunno. He was right behind us."

That was annoying. Where the heck had he gone?

"Ru," Charlie said, shaking my arm. "You can think about boys later. Right now, I need your head in the game, and maybe even your fire power. It might be a good thing that B made himself scarce. He clearly doesn't want to get any more mixed up with our criminal inclinations."

"You're right. I'm focused." I turned my attention back to the blueprint.

"My best bet," Charlie said and tapped the map with her fingernail. "The boiler room. It's the perfect hideout. Sure, it's supposedly closed off, but who knows, right?"

Standing, I dusted myself off and raised my chin. "Come on, then. Let's find our third angel."

21

WE STARED AT THE LARGE STEEL DOOR, CLOSED OFF WITH heavy chains. A collection of signs surrounded the front with clear warnings like 'Danger' and 'Do not enter' written in big letters.

I shared a look with Charlie. "Doesn't look like anyone has gone through here for a while."

"They could have entered through the tunnel system, though," Charlie said, sounding less than confident.

We were both at the end of our ropes, however, and this was our best lead.

"We're going in, then." I stepped forward and tugged at the chain. "You want to borrow a bobby pin again?"

Charlie eyed the padlock. "Don't think that's gonna work on this lock." She stepped backwards. "This one is all yours, I think. I may be Charlie, but I'm no McGee, I'm afraid."

"Come again?"

"Charlie McGee? Firestarter? You haven't read Stephen King?"

I narrowed my eyes at her. I hadn't read that particular book. It was obvious what she meant, however, but I had no idea if I could control it. Up until now, my fire power had been unstable at best. It seemed to manifest whenever I got mad or frustrated.

"Ok," I said. "You should probably move further back."

Charlie complied in a heartbeat, running several feet away from me to hide behind a statue of who I assumed was St. Patrick.

Satisfied with the distance, I reached into the very core of my power, to my blood. Focus, Ruby! My mum's voice whispered through my head: *Focus on your intention, picture what you want to happen, and it shall.* All right, Mum, I'll try this your way.

I lifted my arms forwards, directing my fingers at the lock, and pictured it breaking. The all too familiar feeling of my blood running hotter sent beads of sweat down my spine as the power simmered, then burned to life. I licked my lips, the taste of salt falling on my tongue. Burn, I thought. The fire rushed through me before it shot from my palms in a cascade of tiny fireballs hammering against the lock. The fireballs broke into bursts of flame, exploding against the steel, melting everything. I kept my hands up, and the fire kept coursing out of me while pearls of perspiration dripped down my skin.

Enough, a male voice whispered somewhere at the back of my mind. *Enough now, Princess. Do not let the fire control you. You control it.*

What was that? I recognized the voice from before, but at the same time, I didn't.

The voice was right, however. I fought with all my strength to overpower the fire in me, focusing on what I wanted it to do. It obeyed at last, slinking back inside to the confines of my veins before it stilled entirely.

I dropped to my knees, my breath heavy, but it wasn't like the last time with Shauna. This was more controlled than that had been. It gave me hope that I would learn to wield this power with more confidence the next time around.

Charlie folded her hands on my shoulders, and I sagged backwards. "Are you ok?"

"I am."

"You sure did a number on that door," she chuckled.

My head lifted. The door was completely gone, melted into a puddle of steel that was rapidly turning solid again. It wasn't just the door, however. Half the wall had burned away as well.

"Good thing no one comes to this part of campus very often," Charlie said. "Or they would have seen one heck of a show."

I staggered to my feet, collecting myself. "Well, it's open."

"No doubt about it."

We started forwards and entered the darkness of a long hallway. Fluorescent lights had once been used to light it up, but most of them were broken or covered in cobwebs.

"I can't see anything," Charlie muttered.

"Maybe I can help?" I summoned the fire once again, confident this time. It was a small orb of fire, and I held it securely in my hand, using it to light our way through the hallway. I smiled as I sensed my power bowing to my will, and not frantically lashing out without my say so.

"You're getting good at that." Charlie wiggled her eyebrows. "The boiler room is close, down those stairs, according to the map." She angled her head at an adjoining staircase.

Neither of us said a word as we descended into more darkness, guided by the light source in my hand. If someone was there, we didn't want to alert them to our presence.

The smell of iron crawled up my nose as I planted my feet on the next level. The room in front of us was immense. Four large boilers accompanied several tubes and tanks, alongside machines which I had no idea what they were.

My foot hit something soft, making me stumble forward. I caught myself with my palms, the light evaporating from my hand. Turning back, Charlie had brought her phone out and turned the flashlight on, pointing it between us towards what had made me fall. I backed up on my elbows, and fear clutched at my chest.

Someone—a girl—was lying on the floor at Charlie's feet. I caught a glimpse of the golden hair first. Jen! *Please, no!* I had to find out, so I crawled closer, clutching onto every bit of hope I had before I realized who it was. It wasn't Jen. My relief was short-lived as I recognized the person before me

Diane's open blue eyes stared at me, but there was no sign of life left in them. Her perfect skin had acquired a bluish tint, and parts of her perfect hair had been torn from her scalp, leaving open flesh wounds. She was dead.

The light stirred and I forced myself to look beyond Diane's body and approach my friend. Charlie was shaking, her fear rolling off her.

"We have to move," I whispered.

Charlie sniffled. "I know."

We stepped back over Diane's body to move further into the room. The place made the hairs on my arms stand on end, and the previous warmth I felt turned to ice-cold shivers. A large steel table stood in the middle of the room and I almost gagged. A heap of blood bags was piled on one end, while medical equipment, tubes, a microscope, syringes, vials and equipment I had never seen before were scattered around the wide table. On the other end stood a machine I did recognize, however, as I had seen a similar one at Mum's clinic. A blood centrifuge.

A tug at my arm caught my attention, making me shift my eyes to a ledge up ahead. Someone had been hooked to heavy chains hanging from the roof. Tubes were attached to their bodies with blood bags slowly filling next to them. My fear turned to anger, and my fire sparked up again. Not yet, I demanded, making the fire seethe in my veins until I needed it.

I took Charlie's hand, my eyes adjusting to the dark room.

"I don't think anyone else is here," Charlie managed, her voice breaking.

We found a ladder and climbed to the awning above. Two girls were hanging by their arms, their blood trickling into the tubes.

"Corinne," Charlie whispered, pointing at the nearest girl.

I placed two shaking fingers to her jugular. No pulse. Instinctively, I drew on my healing ability. It was so different from fire. They both came from my blood, but my healing power was soothing, filling me with calm energy and strength. It sifted through me as though gliding on the water before rays of what looked like sunlight radiated from my hands. I placed them over Corinne's heart, willing her to live.

It's too late, Princess. The voice was back again.

"No," I replied. "It can't be."

"Ru, she's gone," Charlie said, yanking my arm. "Someone else needs your help. Someone alive."

That got my attention. I kept the magic rays in my hands as I looked at the next girl.

Jen!

"She's barely breathing." Charlie was sobbing again. "Help her."

Barely, I could work with.

I moved my hands over Jen's body, drawing on the warmth of my healing power. It crashed through me like waves. I couldn't let Jen die, not like Susan. Not like Dad. The energy pulsated wildly through my veins as I pulled the pain from Jen's wounds. It drifted away from her, blending with the scorching light beneath my palms as crimson specks in the otherwise golden hues, patching up the cuts and bruises as I went.

Jen's eyes shot open, and Charlie pulled the needle out from her arm before I sealed that wound as well.

"You're ok," Charlie exclaimed, a bit too loud.

"How do we get you down from there?" I asked, eyeing the chains. I couldn't throw fire at them as I might kill her by doing so. We needed a key.

Jen smiled. "I'll handle that. Thank you for healing me, Ruby. I knew you would save me." She winked, then her hands morphed. White fur spurted from her skin as her limbs changed shape into those of a wolf's. Then she slid her feet—or whatever those were—out of the restraints.

"How?" I mumbled. "Why didn't you do that before."

"I couldn't before. Your healing allowed me to do it now. I'll tell you later because we need to run before they get back."

"They?" Charlie asked.

"Yes. Now, let's get the hell out of Dodge."

I cast a last glance at Corinne's dead body, wishing with all my heart that we had got here sooner, then hurried down the ladder after the others. We sprinted back to the entrance.

It was closed.

"Can't let you leave, ladies," someone said.

I knew that voice.

We spun back on our heels as a light came on by the table to reveal Rahul's face, grinning at us in the glare from the dim light. A door I hadn't seen in the dark was open somewhere at the far end of the room.

"You!" I couldn't believe it.

"Don't look so surprised," he said, picking up a syringe full of blood in his hand. "You're not leaving me, Jen." He blew a kiss at her. She snarled back, long fangs growing out from under her upper lip before my very eyes. She was half-human, half-wolf at this point. "Now, now, ease down, pup. You're valuable, but your friend, she's more valuable than any Mag we've come across."

What? Why would he say that? I stepped backwards until the closed door hugged my back. How was it he thought I was some kind of extra-valuable Magical? I was as common as they came. A half-blood.

"You know," Rahul said. "I thought it was strange that I couldn't find the syringe after losing it during my struggle with Ilyana. As luck would have it, however, I watched you find it. Jen was running around like a fucking bloodhound, way too easy to spot. You, however." He bored his eyes into me again. "You left a drop of blood on a thorn in the rose bush. You really should be more careful with your blood. It's so deliciously rare."

"What is he talking about, Ru?" Charlie asked, her arms clutched around mine.

I shook my head. Parts of what he was saying about Jen being an obvious Shifter made sense. I saw that too, in hindsight, and I should have seen it then. The part about my rare blood, on the other hand, was nothing short of ludicrous.

"Let us go," I said. "There's three of us, and one of you."

"True." Rahul shrugged. "But I'm the one with a syringe full of human blood, not to mention this." He lifted his arm in the air, a gun locked in his grip. "You have magic, sure. Even so, you're not immune to bullets." He gestured at me with the gun to come closer.

I did. What was I supposed to do with him pointing a gun at our faces? The power inside me was stirring with anticipation, waiting for me to make a decision. Still, it wasn't as easy as that. This room was a fire hazard if I ever saw one. One ill-placed fireball and I could set the entire boiler room ablaze. Not to mention the adjacent lecture hall above it that we'd seen on the map.

"Stop," Rahul called. "That's close enough." He directed the gun at my heart as he eased his way towards me. "No sudden moves or I'll shoot to kill."

He raised the syringe, his eyes fixated on the pulsating veins in my arm. Whatever human blood was supposed to do to me, I wasn't going to let him inject me with it. While I was frantically grasping at solutions, the sudden howl of a wolf echoed through the room.

"Duck," Charlie yelled.

I did, and a rush of wind tore at my hair as a large white wolf soared over my head, pinning Rahul to the ground and sending the gun skidding across the floor. The wolf sank its teeth into Rahul's arm as he grabbed for the gun again. Loud growls and snarls ensued as the beast tore into him, blood spraying across the white fur, spilling out on the floor.

"That is enough," a man commanded.

The wolf turned low, and I looked back as well.

Greg Barrows was standing behind Charlie, moving her along with him against the wall. The edge of a knife glinted by Charlie's throat.

"I'm taking this girl with me, and you'll stay where you are or I will slit her throat so deep, it will be impossible to heal her."

"Greg," I hissed, "let her go, and maybe we'll be kind enough to spare your life."

His handsome features contorted into an image of pure evil. His brows deepened over his callous eyes, and his mouth curled into a vicious grin.

"I've killed before," he snarled. "Don't think I won't do it again."

"You mean at the Academy?" I shot back.

"Clever girl." Greg nodded with an approving sneer. "I'm not with them anymore, though."

"I thought no one left the Academy?"

Greg was halfway across the room with Charlie by now. "I guess they found my methods to be too—experimental, even for their standards. But I'm still an asset to them, so they have given me some wiggle room." His lips folded away from his teeth.

I locked eyes with Charlie as they moved into the glow of the table lamp. Tears streamed down her cheeks. There was no way I would let him kill her, but I wasn't about to let him escape either.

You have the power, Princess, the voice in my head called out to me. *You are stronger than you think.*

A wild force of power exploded in my veins, and my skin lit up as the flames licked across my body, filling the room with glowing light.

Greg pressed the knife at Charlie's throat as my arm shot out. A nearly invisible force latched onto his hand, forcing him to drop the knife, before wrapping around his throat. Charlie fell to her knees as Greg lost his grip on her. He wheezed, choking underneath my strength. I wanted him dead.

Jen's wolf form moved in my peripheral vision, rushing over to Charlie, who climbed onto the wolf before it dashed out the back door.

"Please," Greg croaked.

"You don't deserve to live." The sound of my voice boomed as if it was coming from someone else.

Go on, the voice whispered. *It's all within your grasp, Princess.*

I tightened my grip on the magic at my disposal. "What?" I replied. "What is?"

I shook my head from the fog in my mind and stared at Greg's face. He was gasping for every bit of air he could find. This wasn't me.

"No," I shouted. "I'm not doing it." I loosened my grip on him, the flames circling me as I hurried over to Greg to grab his arm. He was unconscious.

"Jen," I yelled.

Seconds later, the white wolf returned.

"Get him out of here. Now! Charlie too. And get as far away as possible."

The wolf tilted its head at me, its large blue eyes looking at me with an unsaid question.

"Yes. We're saving him. But I'm about to blow. I can't stop it. Now, run!"

The wolf bit down on Greg's leg and tossed him over her back before darting off again at an impressive speed.

I curled up in a ball of ever-growing flames. My stomach twisted, my chest expanding with trying to hold my breath to stop the energy from consuming me. Pressing my eyes shut, I wrapped my arms around myself in an effort to stop the fire from exploding.

Let go, Princess, the voice called. *Let go now, or it will implode.*

"*At least I won't blow anything up,*" I said back with my thoughts.

It will kill you, child. Let go now!

Somewhere inside, I knew the voice was telling the truth, and I couldn't hold on much longer. I exhaled sharply and allowed the flames to pull my arms wide, lifting me from the ground to hover in the air. Then I let go. The magical energy blasted out from my body in every direction, a blaze of fire roaring through the room, licking up the walls and across the roof. The flames coiled around me in a storm of fire, swallowing everything in its path. With a snap, the last bit of energy broke free from my skin and I crashed back down with a heavy thud.

22

My heart beat in a slow rhythm, the ground beneath me soft and wet. I rolled to my back and opened my eyes as a tendril of shadow wafted past to disappear into thin air. I sat, staring out at Willow Lake. What in Avalon's Deepest Valleys had just happened?

"Ru?" Jen called.

She came running towards me with bare feet, Charlie's jacket folded around her body, and Charlie sprinting close behind her.

I slapped myself to see if I was dreaming. It hurt, so maybe I wasn't.

How had I not died, though?

The girls threw themselves at me, embracing me tightly.

"I thought you were dead." Charlie was crying. Happy tears this time.

"Nope. Very much alive, it seems." I looked down, my cheeks blossoming with shame. "And very much naked."

Jen laughed. "I know that feeling."

"Here." Charlie offered me her jumper, leaving her with a t-shirt and a pair of jeans.

The jumper was a tad too short, but it covered enough. "Thank heavens you like baggy clothes," I said. Standing warily, everything came rushing back. "Where's Greg?"

"The son of a bitch is in his flat. I injured his leg pretty badly, so he's not about to go anywhere before the police show up."

"You rang them?" I asked.

"Anonymously, but yes." An edge of pride surrounded Jen. For someone who had been held captive for a day, she sure was quick to get back on her feet. Granted, with a little magical juice to help her along.

"But Ru, why would you save him?" Charlie wrapped an arm around me as we walked down the side of the lake.

"I didn't want to become a monster, like him. Something. I don't know, this voice in my head. It saved me, but I also felt like it wanted me to kill Greg. As if it had some sort of weird control over me. I'm not about to let anyone or anything control me ever again."

"I don't know about any voices." Charlie smiled. "But that was one hell of a blast you left behind, Ru."

"Lucky for us, it was contained to the boiler room alone for some reason," Jen added, clearly picking up on my fear. "What I can't understand, though, is how you ended up out here."

"Not sure," I murmured. "I think I may have got some help." I had so many questions, I didn't know where to begin asking, or who to ask.

"First order of business," Jen said, tugging at the bottom of the jacket she was wearing. "We go home and change into something more comfortable."

The jacket was too small for her, so she had it wrapped below her shoulders, though not actually with her arms inside the sleeves.

"I'm with you on that," I said.

We managed to get back to our flat without too many goggling eyes on us, and all three of us changed into sweatpants and our uni jumpers. Being comfortable beat looking good at this point. We huddled up in Jen's bed with our duvets, none of us wanting to be alone.

"Thank you for saving me," Jen said.

"What are friends for?" Charlie squeezed her arms around Jen. "Besides, what would we do without you, hm? We would be completely lost."

"True." Jen laughed.

I stared at her in awe. Looking at her now, it was hard to imagine a large white wolf hiding inside her.

"So," I said. "You're a Shapeshifter."

The laughter stopped, and Jen pulled her hands through her hair, making me think of the white fur of her other persona. "I am, and what exactly are you? I mean, I've known since I first smelled you that you were a Magical, just not exactly what kind."

"She's a Fae," Charlie interjected.

"Fae, huh? Cool. Though, that fire of yours, is that a Fae thing? Don't you all have nurturing kinds of powers?"

"Usually, yes," I said. "The fire is something new."

"Well, you're one tough cookie, that's for sure." Jen leaned back on the wall, folding her hands behind her head. "Me, I come from a long line of wolves, intermingled with humans, of course."

"About that." There was something that had been bothering me, and Jen had said she would tell us later, so why not now? "Why did Rahul want to inject me with human blood?"

"It's what he did to all of us. Well, excluding Diane." Jen sucked on her teeth and sniffled. "She wasn't even a Magical. Her only mistake was having me as her friend. When Rahul took me, she followed us and tried to take him on in the boiler room. A fight she was bound to lose. I couldn't do anything because Rahul had injected me full of human blood and chained me up." A glimpse of anger glinted in her eyes.

Waving a hand in the air, I found myself utterly confused. "So, wait, I don't understand the blood thing."

"Human blood to a Magical lessens our powers. Given enough, they can kill off our magical blood cells altogether, or even kill us in the process. Think of it as a reverse MagX." Jen kicked the duvet off. "We, unlike humans, have a special set of blood cells, which is where the magic comes from. These blood cells are not supposed to survive in a human body but will provide them with powers for a short while until the magical cells more or less die. Sometimes, though, the blood is tainted, or the human takes too much. Then the human dies."

My mouth fell open. "How the—how do you know all this?"

"My mum is a chemist of sorts. She has studied magical blood for most of her life."

We fell silent as Charlie and I crawled underneath

the same duvet. It dawned on me that there was still so much about magic and the magical world I didn't know anything about, even though I had been raised by one of the original Fae descendants.

A police siren pierced the night and we all jumped to our feet at once.

"Let's check it out," Jen said.

"Won't we look suspicious?" I asked.

"Babe, really, half the students will stick their nosy noses into this. We won't be the only ones there."

Jen was right. It would probably be like the last time we had a police visit on campus.

And it was. The students were flocking out to see what was going on. The front of the staff building was crowded with students and staff, everyone trying to get a glimpse of why the police were there. A group of officers was already rolling out a band of yellow tape to stop people from stepping into what appeared to be a crime scene. Three police cars and an ambulance were parked outside.

I peeked past a couple of guys in front of me, not tall enough to see over their heads. My body stiffened as two paramedics carried Greg out on a stretcher, deservedly in handcuffs. Officer Paddock ascended last. He shifted his gaze around the crowd, and somehow his eyes locked onto mine. Should I run? No, that would look wildly suspicious.

Paddock exchanged a few words with the paramedics and the other officer before he ducked under the yellow tape and pushed his way through the crowd to us.

"Ladies," Paddock said. "Care to join me?"

We followed him back under the yellow tape and to his car where we were out of earshot of prying spectators.

The icy cold stare of Paddock's eyes shifted between us. "I see you found your friend."

"Turns out, she was at a mate's place, phone battery dead and all," Charlie said. "We were worried about nothing. The missing girls put us on edge."

"Rightly so," Paddock said. "You can rest easy now, however, as I can already confirm that the evidence we've found is enough to put that leech of a man—" He angled his head towards Greg, who was receiving medical attention at the ambulance. "Behind lock and key for a very long time."

Uncomfortable, I took Charlie's hand. "Thank you, Officer Paddock," I said. "May we leave now?"

"You may."

We hurried away from the scene and away from the crowd, heading for the lake.

A thought struck me, and a sudden fear rose in my chest. "What if he tells them about you, Jen? Or me, for that matter."

"Oh no," Charlie exclaimed. "What if he does?"

A few leaves rustled in the wind, sailing down onto the water.

"I don't think he will," Jen murmured. "I mean, he could, and that would be catastrophic. Still, I don't think so. I may or may not have threatened to sic a pack of wolves on him if he said anything."

"Jeannine Lune!" I said, gawking.

She shrugged. "I'd be more worried if and when he is set free.

I nodded.

"But if he dares to show his face again, the wolfpack might pay him an actual visit." Jen's lips curled into a feral grin.

Her confidence washed over me, and without knowing why, I believed she was right. Either way, it was too late to do anything about it now. I had decided to save his miserable life, and it was the right decision. Rahul, on the other hand, was gone, burned to nothing but ashes most likely. I glanced at Jen. That was something she would have to live with, and I didn't envy her one bit, but it had been self-defence, and I would make sure I told her that until she believed she had done the right thing. Whatever came next, we would deal with it then. If nothing else, we had delivered the culprit, and it was over. At least the mystery of the missing girls had been solved.

Me, I had a whole lot of other mysteries to deal with.

"Hey," someone called from behind the white willow.

"Duncan?" Charlie asked.

Duncan stepped out from behind the tree, his hands in his pockets and his chin hanging to his chest.

Charlie ran over and flung her arms around him. "I'm so happy to see you're safe."

"You're not mad?" He sidestepped out of Charlie's arms.

"Of course I am." Charlie slapped him amicably on his shoulder. "But I can be happy that you're alive at the same time. I'll be mad at you later."

He gave us all a half-smile and fell in step as we walked back to Craydon Court.

As angry as we might be with him, I was also feeling guilty about ever suspecting him of being a killer. Apologies would be served all around.

Not tonight, though. Tonight we were safe, and together.

23

EARLY MORNINGS WERE QUIET ON CAMPUS. BRADY'S WASN'T open yet, and most students were probably still in bed. The wind brushed my face as I ran, Maroon 5 singing about "Girls Like You" in my ears, which I gladly took to heart. It had been a couple of days since Greg Barrows was arrested, and we hadn't heard anything from the police on the matter after our little chat with Paddock. Perhaps the janitor had kept his mouth shut about Jen and me after all. The explosion in the boiler room had been written off as an accident due to poor maintenance, and no one had said anything about Rahul.

Then there was poor Diane. Her parents had arrived yesterday, and Brendan had gone to talk to them as I couldn't bring myself to do it after her lifeless eyes had haunted me in my sleep. Also, I felt like an idiot for having been jealous of her. On my bed at this very moment lay a special fencing outfit, with a ruby embroidered on the chest and my name on the back. It wasn't up to competition standards, according to Brendan, but he wanted me to have something special for when he was going to teach me some moves, and Diane had helped him to arrange it. That was what they had been discussing when Professor Kaine spotted them. I had never thought about trying fencing in my life, but now I wanted to. Both because of Brendan, and because of Diane.

The White Willow University gates whisked past me as I picked up the pace, leaving campus behind me. After about five minutes, I turned left into Richmond Park, as the band in my headset finished the song aptly named 'Closure'.

I slowed my run and jogged down to the riverbed, where I stretched my limbs for a few minutes before taking off my shoes and socks to sit. The water enveloped my feet as I sank them below the surface. I fished out my phone and swiped open the caller section to find Brendan's picture. It was way too early to give him a ring, but what the heck. He deserved it for bailing on us, even if I was kind of glad he had.

It rang for a while, then went to voicemail. Yep, too early. Swiping down the list again, I pressed the picture of Mum. She was an early bird like me.

Sure enough, Mum picked up at the third ring. "Good morning, love," she said brightly.

"Mum," I said. "It's so good to hear your voice."

"You're out running?"

"I am."

"I'm happy to hear that you've not stopped doing the things you'd do at home. Running has always cleared your head. Your dad was the same way. Although, there are other things I'm not so happy about."

Her tone changed from warm to strict, and I already knew what was coming. It had been all over the news yesterday. I had simply been too much of a chicken to tell her anything. Sitting here by myself like this, though, I felt more at ease, and I also had some questions only Mum could answer.

"I know. I meant to give you a ring yesterday," I lied. "There was just a lot of stuff going on, and I had a paper to hand in. My first one."

"Mind telling me about the so-called Willow murderer I've been reading about. I was close to jumping on the first train down the moment I heard about it. I knew it was a bad idea sending you to London."

"I know, Mum, and I get it. But I'm here now."

I understood better than she knew, a lot better than I had before as well, but I wasn't giving her the whole truth. That would get me shipped back to Cheshire before I could spell the word Magic.

"The culprit was caught, though. He's gone. Nothing to worry about anymore."

"He killed three girls, sweetheart. You can't blame me for worrying."

"I don't, I'm just saying it's over. He's gone, and I'm really settling in. I've found great friends here, the kind of friends I've never had before. You'll love them, I know you will."

Hesitating, I wondered how much I should share. It wasn't as if Mum would spill anyone's dirty laundry. She was a master of keeping secrets. "And in fact, Jen, she—well, she's a wolf."

"What? You mean she's a Shapeshifter?"

231

I pulled my feet out of the water to let them dry on the grass, before falling back to face the sky. "Yes. A quite impressive one, too."

"Then I suppose she knows about you as well?"

Crap. I hadn't thought that far. "Yes, Mum. She does, but it's not like I told her, she could smell it on me apparently."

Mum chuckled. "Shifters are cunning like that. But Ruby—" Her tone changed again. "Shifters are also known to be reckless, stubborn creatures. I know she's your friend, and you like her, but even so, I must advise caution. The wolf-shifters especially have a rather— violent history."

"I promise. Jen is cool, though. You'll like her, I know you will." While I was on the truth train, I decided to ride it for a bit longer. "Mum—"

"What is it, love?" It was as if she could sense the anxiety in my heart.

"Something's been happening to me lately. I keep hearing this voice in my head, and I've been seeing a man."

Mum's breathing quickened on the other end. "Seeing a man? You mean Brendan?"

"No, not that kind of seeing. More like a shadow—or a man in the shadows. It's hard to explain. Whatever it is, it appears friendly, but I don't know, it kind of scares me, too," I admitted and held my breath for a moment. That might have been oversharing.

Mum sighed heavily into the phone. "Ruby Guinevere Morgan, you listen very carefully to what I have to say. Do not, under any circumstances engage with this— thing. Stay as far away as you can. If it talks to you, don't answer. If the shadows reach for you, walk away. And if you find yourself unable to do so, call upon your Fae powers, shield yourself, and the shadows will retreat. I promise."

"You know what it is?"

A long pause ensued, where all I could hear was Mum's breathing. What must have been a minute went by before she spoke again.

"I do know what this is, and I wish I could tell you more, though this is not something we can talk about over the phone. I promise to tell you everything when you come home for vacation or when I come to visit you in London. Whichever comes first. For now, just remember what I've said. It may appear friendly, and it may whisper strange things in your ear, but do not believe a thing it says. Stay away from it. I don't think it would physically harm you, but it can do a lot more damage than that."

I thought I had heard her scared when we talked about the Academy, but this? This was beyond even that. It was clear she needed reassurance on the matter, so I decided to give it to her. And I would try my best to keep this particular promise.

"Ok, Mum. I promise."

We spoke for a while longer, both of us trying to ease the tension that had built increasingly throughout the beginning of our chat. I had more questions to ask her, like why Rahul seemed to think my blood was so special, but Mum seemed completely out of sorts after my mention of the shadowy figure, and telling her about Rahul would mean telling her about the boiler room, which was definitely a big no.

So we chatted about Kit and the clinic. Nice and normal things. Then we hung up.

I put my socks and shoes on and was walking back to the path when it felt as if something was breathing down my neck.

I took a sharp turn. There it was again, on the other side of the lake, watching me. Tendrils of silver and black licked the air around the shadowy figure inside. Mum's warning sent alarm bells through my mind, and yet, there was something about the shadows that drew me towards it. I had made a promise to Mum, however, so I tore myself away from the spot and ran.

Daring a glance over my shoulder, the shadow was still there, so I kept running until I could no longer see it when I turned.

Whatever it was, Mum had better tell me everything.

BOOK TWO

SENTRIES OF CAMELOT

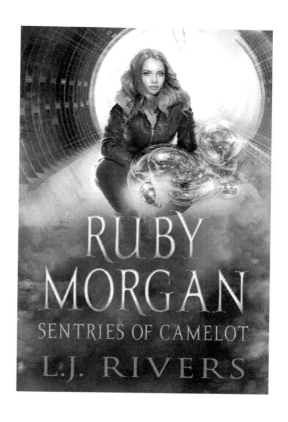

Printed in Great Britain
by Amazon